AUCTIONED

#1

CARA DEE

Copyright © 2018 by Cara Dee
All rights reserved

This book is licensed for your personal enjoyment and may not be reproduced in any way without documented permission of the author, not including brief quotes with links and/or credit to the source. Thank you for respecting the hard work of this author. This is a work of fiction and all references to historical events, persons living or dead, and locations are used in a fictional manner. Any other names, characters, incidents, and places are derived from the author's imagination. The author acknowledges the trademark status and owners of any word-

COPYRIGHT

marks mentioned in this work of fiction. Characters portrayed in sexual situations are 18 or older.

Edited by Silently Correcting Your Grammar, LLC.
Formatted by Eliza Rae Services.
Proofread by Tanja.

Auctioned
A SERIES WITHIN THE CAMASSIA COVE UNIVERSE

Camassia Cove is a town in northern Washington created to be the home of some exciting love stories. Each novel taking place here is a standalone, with the exception of sequels, and they will vary in genre and pairing. What they all have in common is the town in which they live. Some are friends and family. Others are complete strangers. Some have vastly different backgrounds. Some grew up together. It's a small world, and many characters will cross over and pay a visit or two in several books. But, again, each novel stands on its own, and spoilers will be avoided as much as possible.

Auctioned is the first book of a new series taking place in the Camassia Cove universe, and **all five books will center around Gray and Darius**. It is not required to read previous Camassia novels to get the full enjoyment of this one, but if you're interested in keeping up with secondary characters, the town, the timeline, and future novels, check out Camassia Cove's own page www.caradeewrites.com. There you will also see which characters have gotten their own books already as well as which books are in the works.

Thank you

Eliza, Lisa, my kickass crew, Rob, Tanja, and the best readers a scribbler could ask for.

Prologue

Gray grinned to himself as he scrolled through baby clothes on his phone. Online shopping was dangerous when you'd learned you were expecting your first niece or nephew, and his funds were limited. He couldn't help it, though. He was stoked for his stepsister—and, frankly, himself. He was gonna spoil that kid rotten.

Taking a left on Sixth Street, he looked up briefly to make sure shopping for baby socks wasn't getting him lost on the way home. He could picture his friends and brothers ribbing him about that for years.

It'd gotten dark while Gray had been to the movies with a couple friends. He was almost home, thankfully. Summer was over, and he was one of the last to haul out the fall wardrobe. Probably time to start using a jacket. Northern Washington wasn't known for its heat.

"Hey!" Gray banged furiously against the planks that boarded up the window. Between the cracks, he could see a man exiting a car across the street, and it was the first person Gray had seen all day. "Help! Over here!" With a growl of frustration and panic, he tried to dig his fingers between two boards to get them loose. "Up here!" He kept going, even as his fingers started bleeding from the rough splinters.

His stomach churned as he heard the heavy footfalls of the two men who lived in this house. Or so he guessed. He hadn't paused to consider ownership of the shitty little house on a street he didn't recognize.

"Just silence him," one of the men snarled on the other side of the door.

Flight was out, so Gray steeled himself to fight. His chest heaved, his fists clenched. And the second the locks were turned and the door opened, he charged with every bit of strength he possessed.

A message popped up on Gray's phone as he was crossing the park behind the community college.

I want to celebrate my birthday with you. Please say yes, beautiful.

Gray wanted to. Fuck, did he want to spend that day with Craig. But he'd drawn the line. It'd been nearly three years of texting and confessing feelings and fantasies, three years of not being intimate with the man he loved. He knew if he spent any alone time with Craig now, he'd cave.

His thumb hovered over the send button, reading and rereading his reply, then eventually fired it off.

Leave your wife first.

A strong wind rustled the trees above him and sent a shiver down his spine. Fall was really here. He zipped up his hoodie and bunched his shoulders. The apartment he shared with a couple teammates and too much hockey gear to stumble over was just around the little duck pond. He hoped he could fall asleep quickly tonight, 'cause being reminded of Craig's birthday sucked.

Gray could thank—or curse—his mom for putting so much value on morals. High motherfucking morals. He shook his head and wished he could just, for one damn night, get what he wanted. A stolen moment. Technically, they'd already had one. A kiss—a heated, awesome kiss—right after Craig became Craig and stopped being Coach Fuller.

As Gray nursed his no doubt fractured wrist, he counted the cracks in the ceiling. The pain had lessened to a low throb after keeping it still for two days, and the swelling had gone down.

He knew a thing or two about fractures, being a hockey player. Unlike his younger twin brothers, he didn't dream of making it in the NHL, though. Same with Gray's best friend, Abel, who played for the Canucks in Vancouver. No, Gray wanted to coach or work with kids in some other capacity. But all of that hurt to think about now.

Rolling onto his side, he winced as his joints protested. The thin mattress was the only thing in the room, aside from a portable toilet in the opposite corner. More often than not, his eyes strayed to the boarded-up window, which beat staring at the faded wallpaper.

Six days. That was how long it'd been since he was taken. Long enough for him to become a case. First as a missing person, then with the suspicion of foul play. Had he made the news yet? Most likely. In fact, Gray counted on it, because he wasn't the first to disappear from their little town. A boy had gone missing earlier this year, followed by a young woman a couple months ago.

He screwed his eyes shut and willed himself not to cry. It would do him no good.

With his apartment building in sight, he picked up the pace and—

A screeching sound broke his train of thought, and Gray looked around, confused. This area was usually dead at night, unless it was a Friday or Saturday and fellow students threw a party or four.

He was supposed to have graduated last semester, but failing grades had forced him to retake a few classes.

A black sedan rolled up right outside the building, blocking Gray's path. A big man stepped out and asked, "Are you Gray Nolan?"

Gray stiffened, torn between worry and suspicion. "What do you want with him?"

The man cracked a grin that revealed perfectly white teeth, except one was missing.

Another man was quick to join the first one, and they exchanged a sentence in a language Gray couldn't understand or identify.

A beat later, they both flew at Gray.

01

Gray could picture his mom's face in the most idyllic scenarios. He could envision her laughing as she walked down the sloped lawn behind the inn she ran. The sun shining, the wind catching in her long, dark hair, the apple trees in bloom. Perhaps Gray had told her an inappropriate joke, and she was doing her mom thing by pretending not to find it funny. She'd look up at him with narrowed eyes, even as they danced with mirth, and scold him for his language or something. Then a giggle would slip free, and the laughs would follow.

Maybe it was because she'd had kids young that Gray was so close with her. The mama bear was always lurking and ready to pounce, but for the most part, they were friends. He helped out at the inn whenever he had the time, working side by side with his mother when most guys his age would rather chill with buddies.

The memory of his mom's mischievous smirks and soft laughter were among Gray's favorites, but they were always interrupted by the harsh reality. Her happiness grew distorted before morphing into despair and anguish-laden rage. Gray imagined her surrounded by law enforcement as she tried to figure out where her second eldest son had gone. She was such a short little thing. A complete sweetheart, until you messed with her.

The van jostled, bringing Gray out of his head. The air was humid and pungent, reeking of mildew, piss, and vomit. His restraints were cutting into his skin, and the burlap sack covering his head was thick and scratchy.

Find me, Mom. Please find me.

"Stand still!" The motherfucker fisted Gray's hair through the rough material of the bag that covered his head and positioned him on the scale. "One-eighty-nine. Gotta love the athletes. He'll go for a lot."

Gray gnashed his teeth together.

This isn't real, this isn't real.

He wasn't going to be sold. It seemed as impossible now as it had the first time he'd been told of his fate. That shit didn't happen, not in America.

Bob claimed otherwise. Men without faces and names had come and gone in the weeks Gray had been God knows where, except for one man. He had a craggy face and crooked teeth, and on the eighth day in a shitty little house with faded wallpaper, he'd strolled into what was left of Gray's life, grinned widely, and said, "Call me Bob."

Bob made Gray's life a living hell.

Another man grunted. "The fit ones also escape easier. Measurements next."

Every digit imaginable was jotted down. From Gray's six feet in height to...Jesus Christ, the length of his flaccid cock. Bob and who Gray assumed was a physician spoke as if they were the only people in the room.

"Tattoos or scars?" Doc asked. "Eye color, hair color... Anything that stands out?"

Bob ripped off the burlap sack, and Gray blinked at the

harsh light. His eyes burned and watered rapidly. A blurry face obstructed his view, and there was a painful grip on his jaw.

"Light brown hair. Blue eyes, I guess. No scars—wait." He gripped Gray's bicep next. "Four-inch scar across his neck, several fainter ones on his torso. No ink, no piercings, handful of smaller birthmarks on his back and chest."

Doc hummed and walked closer. Gray's eyes wouldn't fucking stop running; he hadn't seen daylight—artificial or otherwise—for more than a few seconds at a time in weeks. Ever since he'd been moved from the house.

Doc poked a pen at the scars along Gray's ribcage. "What sport, boy?" This guy had a Southern accent. He was old, bald, and short.

"Fuck you," Gray gritted out.

That earned him a bitch slap that sent his head sideways. The pain didn't even register.

Bob laughed under his breath.

"Hockey," Gray muttered at Doc's impatient look. Then he wrenched his gaze away and took in the dank office.

There was an old newspaper sticking up from the trash can, but he couldn't see if it was local or anything.

"Violent sport," Doc tsked. "How old are you?"

"Twenty." Blinking past the stinging, Gray continued to search the office for clues. He spotted a calendar on the wall that made him sick. *November*. "Twenty-one."

He'd missed his birthday. He'd also been gone for over two months.

Doc narrowed his eyes.

"It's true," Bob said. "He's twenty-one."

Gray was stuck on the month. *November, November, November*. He'd suspected they were no longer in Washington—or even Oregon—and now he knew it for certain. The weather outside was too warm for November.

He couldn't imagine how his mom was faring.

Every time he thought of his family, the grief nearly did him in. It spread like fire through his veins, making it hard for him to breathe.

"Has he tried to escape?" Doc asked.

"Three times," Bob grunted in reply.

Doc wasn't happy about that, and he asked his next question while making another note. "Did he ever get close?"

Once. Gray swallowed bile. It was when two men had escorted him from that house he'd spent the first two weeks in... Gray had gotten loose from his restraints and tried to run.

Bob had caught up with him, and later that night, he'd made Gray regret he was alive.

"Hello?"

Gray shut his eyes and stopped moving around inside the wooden box. He couldn't stretch out his legs, and the top of his head touched the ceiling. Rolling his shoulders and twisting his body was often all he could do to stop the numbness from growing too painful.

He wasn't alone in the back of the truck. Judging by the sounds and the voices sometimes reaching out, he guessed there were around nine of them right now. All men. Or boys... Always leaving one storage unit or garage bay to go to another.

"Try to get some sleep," Gray croaked.

"You never answer," the boy whispered. "I'm scared."

Gray scrubbed tiredly at his face, ashamed because he did, in fact, avoid talking to anyone. It made the guys real. Some of them sounded so fucking young, and Gray was scared out of his mind too. He couldn't be strong for others who might need him to.

"I know." His head hit the side of the large crate, and he blinked. Sometimes, there were slivers of light he could follow. Nothing now, though. Everything was pitch black.

A thin film of slime covered parts of the crates. Bodily fluids and mildew.

The boy coughed softly. "Are you maybe from Camassia Cove in Washington?"

Gray frowned. "Why?"

"I heard a guard mention it at the last place," he revealed. "I'm from there too."

Gray released a breath. "When were you taken?" Was this the kid who'd gone missing at the beginning of the year?

"I don't know, a few weeks ago."

Oh. So, after Gray had been kidnapped.

He didn't wanna think about it—or anything that involved their home. It was too painful and brought forth too many memories. He missed his family so fucking much. Gage, his big brother. Gabriel and Gid, his younger twin brothers. And Mom and Isla and his stepdad and…everyone. Friends—especially Abel. *Craig.* Fuck, his chest hurt. Wounded feelings from before mingled with love, combined with the increasing aches and the horror of being abducted. Jesus Christ, literally *abducted.* These things happened on the news! Or in movies.

"My name is Milo," the boy said nervously.

Gray scrubbed at his face, the rope around his wrists cinching tighter. Now the boy had a name. It changed things.

"Does anyone know where we are?" another guy asked.

Fuck no. Gray snapped his mouth shut. He'd been through this before. Shortly after he was taken, he'd been in a truck with four others. They'd established names and birthplaces, all trying to piece details together. Then everyone was taken away, maybe in a different truck going someplace else or…fuck if Gray knew. The next time, there'd been a couple girls too.

He loathed thinking about what happened to them when they were suddenly shipped like cattle to another destination. It made him wonder how big this whole thing was. Could he call it a network? Organized slavery? *Human trafficking.* The term hit him like a bolt, and it wrenched a pained breath from him.

Trafficking was invisible, yet, somehow, always a word on politicians' lips. Sometimes, Gray would hear about it on the news, trafficking rings being exposed and blown up, but it was a crime so heinous it was impossible to grasp. Like anyone else, he'd think how horrible trafficking was. When leaders rallied before elections, saying they had to fight the drug trade and human trafficking, everyone went *hell yeah.* Because who wouldn't? No one stood up and said the war on drugs wasn't important.

As Gray listened to the guys making wary introductions, it terrified him to think how big this could be. He envisioned a dark map lighting up with a neon grid that grew denser and more heavily trafficked, and no one knew. The men and women passing the truck he was in had no clue. Like him, they'd seen news segments. Young girls, often. Always far away. Not in the truck next to them. To them, the grid remained invisible.

How many locations had he been taken to? Twelve? Thirteen? During overnight stays, he was locked in his crate. He could only hear the nightmares of others.

Gray was jostled awake. At the first assault of a simple flashlight, he hissed and cowered away in a corner. *Welcome to another night of terror.* Knees pulled up, tied hands covering his face. Light burned. The familiar smell of piss and vomit mingled with salt... That sparked something, and he took a tentative whiff. *Ocean.* He could smell the ocean. Or was he imagining it?

"Wake up!" It was the driver, and soon, more light filled the truck. Bearable light, Gray guessed, in comparison to the sun. He wasn't sure he could live through a sunrise at this point. His eyes only knew the flickering lights of garage bays and the sharp, white beams from flashlights. "Crate four and six," the driver told someone. "Food for the others."

Two crates were lifted off the truck, and Gray prayed he could forget the heartbreaking sound of young men begging for their lives.

How many weeks had passed now?

Packets of rice and steamed vegetables were shoved in between the cracks of the crates—the same every night. Then they'd be back on the road for a few hours, only to make a final stop before a new day began. At that stop, they'd be hauled out of their boxes and hosed down. If anyone got mouthy, which Gray had learned the hard way, their one and only bathroom visit was taken away, and they got to experience waterboarding.

He flinched at a certain memory but managed to shove it aside.

"On your feet, slave."

Gray shuddered violently as someone guided him roughly out of the truck. There was a bag over his head again. The telltale beep to alert that the lift gate was in use, the low murmur of voices around, boys wondering what was going on, the lift gate lowering with him on it—Gray could anticipate all of it.

He stood stock-still on the concrete ground and waited for the water. Every shuffle and noise registered, and then it hit him. The blast of cold water. He sucked in a breath and squeezed his eyes shut harder. One boy cried out. If the low-life scum were feeling extra sadistic, the first attack of the hose would hit the boys right in the face. Not even the burlap could shield them from the force of the frigid water.

They were deemed clean when teeth were chattering and their bodies shaking.

A quick bathroom break entailed being shoved into a porta-potty where the men got two minutes at best to relieve themselves. It was the only time their wrists weren't shackled or bound. After which, they stumbled out and felt a gun pressing to their heads.

Gray was beginning to take comfort from the burlap sack. He didn't wanna see the hell he lived through.

Soon enough, he was shoved back into his crate, another night drawing to a close.

Like the doctor's exam, a rare night here and there stood out. Tonight, Gray and the other young men were shuffled out of the truck and into another garage bay, bags thrown over their heads, but there was no hose waiting for them, nor had they been fed yet. Instead, they were all ordered on their knees with their heads bowed.

Panic seized Gray's chest. *Is this it? Have they gone through all this to give me a bullet in the head?* Just like that, his rational side kicked in. There wasn't a chance in hell they were gonna kill him after everything. He'd been manhandled by countless men throughout this time, and they probably didn't do it for free. An operation like this had to be costly.

"Please don't kill me," one guy sobbed.

He was new.

"Disappointingly little money in selling corpses," a man said impassively. "Start with him, Gregor."

Gray's ears prickled. He strained to be alert, refusing to let the fatigue get the best of him. Boots scraped the cement. Wherever they stopped, it wasn't near Gray. This time.

"This the final eight for Joulter?" someone asked in a gravelly voice.

"Yes. We'll get the other six tomorrow."

The next thing that registered was a low, jagged buzz. The first words that flew into Gray's head were *tattoo gun*. Confirmed by a boy whimpering in pain and a motherfucker telling him to be still. Gray tensed up and steeled himself. *They're gonna mark me. They're gonna put a mark on me.* Milo was next, and Gray listened to his shaky breaths as the boy tried to be brave. Each faint, choking sound was a stab in Gray's chest.

"One of them was reserved, right?" It was the gravelly voice again.

"This one," another replied, and it was followed by a pained sound. "He's to be delivered with a chip already. Buyer ain't takin' any chances, I guess."

Gray's mind was quick to draw conclusions. Chip. GPS or something else that would track the kid. Making it almost impossible to escape. On the other hand, Gray and the other six *wouldn't* be chipped. He would only need a small window. If he saw a chance to run, he would. *Saw*, being the ironic keyword. With a bag over his head, he didn't see a whole lot.

A meaty hand clamped down on Gray's neck through the scratchy fabric, and Gray clenched his jaw. This was it. He'd get some kind of mark—a permanent one. Unsurprisingly, it didn't faze him more than the other abuse. He could survive a tattoo. Being kidnapped, maybe not.

The buzz grew louder, and the bag over Gray's head was pushed up enough to expose the back of his neck. What followed was a trail of fire that pierced his skin. He broke out in a sweat, the pain reverberating in his skull and locking his jaw into place. He gnashed his teeth so hard he thought he was gonna crush them.

Something was different.

"Be quiet, Milo." Gray spoke the words under his breath, too caught up in the outside world to try consoling Milo again. "*Please.* Something's—" Shit, he didn't even know what to say. As the truck turned, so did Gray. He twisted his upper body inside the crate, as if he could suddenly see through walls just because he was facing the right direction.

His neck strained, reminding him of the no doubt infected, two-day-old brand. Right now, he couldn't bring himself to care. For the past hour or so, the truck had driven in a strange pattern. Bumpier roads, frequent turns. Hope was the last thing that died, Gray had read somewhere. And he couldn't help but wonder if the sharp turns and detours meant that the driver was trying to shake someone. Someone following them, maybe.

After a while, the truck slowed down.

"Joulter cargo!" The voice of the driver was muffled through a wall but distinct nonetheless. Another voice replied, and this time, Gray couldn't decipher the words. "No, the midnight departure with the queer boys."

Gray's back straightened and became rigid, and he hit his head on the ceiling of the crate. *Queer boys.* Oh fuck. "Milo." He rushed out the silently crying boy's name. "Are you gay?"

"I am," someone else croaked.

"Me too."

Milo sniffled. "Yeah?"

"Damn," Gray whispered.

There was one guy Gray's age—Cole—who'd traveled with them for maybe a week. He spoke up next. "Special requests from buyers." His guess confirmed Gray's fear. Every time they'd traveled with others, it'd been different legs of different journeys. Girls, boys, straight, gay; somehow, they were categorized, whether it was by sexuality, gender, body shape, or skin color.

Gray thought back on the glimpses of the guys he was with. Sexuality established: gay. All of them athletic and cut but not bulky. All on the young side. Gray and Cole were the eldest, if he wasn't mistaken. *We're the fucking twinks*. He glared at nothing, vaguely offended. He didn't look like a stereotypical bottom boy, goddammit.

With a shake of his head, he thought further, mainly on how these people-harvesting criminals knew so much. They didn't snatch victims at random, and Gray didn't advertise his sexuality. *Much*. His friends knew and had zero problems; still, he was heavily involved in hockey, so he chose not to flaunt anything. He was also single—officially. Only one man would hopefully dispute that status. Regardless...no one would know he was gay unless they either knew him personally or...if they'd found his Facebook.

It sent chills down his spine to realize they'd been watching him.

It would explain how Bob had known his age. They'd fucking spied on Gray.

"We have to run," he said quickly. Panic rose at the thought of not getting any more chances. "If we've reached the destination where they'll try to sell us, we gotta try to escape—by any means necessary."

"I'm in. We can't afford to hesitate," Cole said in his Southern accent. "Charlie, you can't even try. They'll know where you are." That was the boy with a GPS chip embedded under his skin. "The rest of us—soon as we get a chance, we run."

Gray nodded to himself. "Don't wait for anyone. We have a bigger shot if one slips away and calls the police."

It was an unstable agreement among Cole, Gray, and six boys who were so afraid that their every breath was shaky or thick with emotion.

If Gray had to choose between a life in captivity and death…

Light exploded around them as the door was opened, and Gray snuck closer to the boards. Blinking rapidly past the burn, he searched for clues and escape routes. He needed to be alert, because if that tiny window of opportunity appeared, he wasn't gonna waste a millisecond.

His heart thundered in his chest as two men headed straight for his crate. Feet firmly planted on the floor, knees pulled up, he summoned all his strength. Which wasn't much, but he had the element of surprise, and he could shoot up quickly in this position.

When he spotted one of the men gripping a shotgun tightly, his heart plummeted, though he remained determined. Childhood memories flashed by, and he swallowed hard. Life wasn't supposed to end here. Not like this. It wasn't fucking fair.

"Rise and shine, fuckboy." A guard turned the key in the three locks that held the crate shut, then lifted the lid just enough to shove in the barrel of a shotgun. Opening the lid farther, the guard flashed a wide smirk. A scar slashed across his cheek and created a deep crease whenever his mouth twisted. "Turn around."

"Why the fuck would I?" Gray spat out. Rage engulfed him, and he balled his hands into fists. His lungs squeezed.

He chuckled. "I think you're smart enough to know we won't kill you, but there are other ways to use a shotgun. Would you like it shoved up your ass?"

Gray swallowed, and against everything he wanted, he shuffled around inside the crate so he had his back to them. This wasn't how he was gonna find his escape.

"See? Obedient already. Your owner will like you." Next, there was a hand on his neck, and then a sharp sting. Gray's eyes widened. It dawned on him as quickly as the sedative kicked in. They were putting him down like a goddamn dog in order to move...him...

"Fucking...bastards," Gray groaned. The hatred blazed inside of him, even as his limbs grew heavy and his mind sluggish.

"Wake up! All yours, sir." A bucket of cold water was thrown over Gray's lifeless body, and he jolted awake. His head swam, shock held him in invisible bondage, and he was so disoriented that his eyes crossed and rolled back. There was no scratchy bag to shield his face, or rather, his eyes. Light exploded. A moan of pain slipped through his lips. He was rocking, or swaying—either way, the ground was unsolid.

The sound of calm waves registered.

The smell of the ocean, much stronger than last time.

Sea gulls. The *sun*.

"Ow..." He whimpered and shut his eyes. Even behind closed lids, the light was brilliant and white.

Before he knew it, someone was scrubbing him clean with gentle strokes. The sponge was soft and smelled of sandalwood and fresh soap. He couldn't move an inch, no matter how hard he tried. Instead, he rolled with the movements and pushes of the person washing him and what he presumed was a boat.

The air was fresh. He couldn't decide if it was crisp or humid. Maybe it was morning.

Definitely not in Washington.

No, this was the heat of summer in November. Or December now, he guessed.

The person who cleaned him spoke, his voice impossibly angelic. "Welcome to Miami."

"I—" Gray couldn't speak. He could barely form a coherent thought, but he managed to crack one eye open and squint. "Are..." *you here to save us?* The man couldn't be more than twenty, and he looked so sweet, so innocent, and so *pretty*. His hair was the blackest black, his skin paler than snow, and Gray had never seen eyes that light blue before.

"Don't speak, sweetling." The guy cupped Gray's cheek briefly, then returned to dragging the sponge over his body. "Everything will be fine. My name is Vanya, and I'll take care of you."

It was too much for Gray to process. He didn't know if this was good or bad, so he sort of checked out.

Sometime later, he knew it was bad. The guy named Vanya had merely cleaned him up, given him a pair of white briefs, shaved his scruff, and put some shit in his hair to make it look shiny. A guard had taken over from there, and he'd brought Gray to the other guys, who'd undergone the same pre-auction makeover. Bruises had been covered, a few cuts had been cleaned, and the cabin they were locked inside smelled of disinfectants.

Along the walls of the otherwise completely empty cabin, all eight guys were shackled to metal hooks.

Their hope of escape had been shot straight to hell before they could even try.

The defeat crushed Gray. When the other guys made an effort to gather information on their new whereabouts, he stayed silent. They were on an opulent yacht, he learned. At least four decks. They were surrounded by water. Tight security with big men patrolling heavily armed. Milo had heard whispers about "buyers boarding at midnight," and another guy had heard they were anticipating a bidding war for two of the boys.

Cole was an attractive guy who looked like a quarterback, complete with rich, brown hair and matching eye color. He was a realist too, and he guessed the two youngest boys—Milo and Jackie—would be popular.

That frightened Milo. "What makes you say that? I'm nothing special." Maybe he wasn't. He was scrawnier and fair-skinned, though his green eyes and dark, shaggy hair would probably draw a crowd. However, it was his age. He was sixteen.

"You're jailbait on a boat that'll be full of perverts," Cole replied grimly.

Jackie bit his lip and turned to the wall, shivering in fear. Unlike Milo, Jackie was tall, blond, and blue-eyed. But he shared the same innocence, and he was only seventeen.

The door suddenly swung open, and all the guys whipped their heads around to see a voluptuous woman enter the cabin. Her presence was immense, and somehow she came off as more dangerous than the two men flanking her. Blood-red hair, matching her lipstick and long nails. A leather dress with a corset pushed her big breasts together. Yet, it was her eyes Gray got stuck on. Pale blue and shaped like almonds, like that Vanya guy. They had to be related.

She didn't speak. Taking measured steps, she went from guy to guy to inspect them from head to toe and back up. Gray tensed his jaw as she paused in front of him. Her full lips twisted in amusement.

"Lower him to two hundred," she murmured absently. "Maybe a shooter will want him."

What the fuck did that mean?

She cocked her head. "My son has taken a liking to you. I don't see it." *Vanya*. Jesus Christ, they were mother and son.

"You won't be easy to handle." With a dismissive wave, she continued to the next guy, and Gray let out a breath.

The word shooter went on repeat. It sure as hell didn't sound like a good thing.

The entire day was a mindfuck. Absolutely nothing happened. They remained shackled to the wall in the empty cabin, and after Red had left with her security, no one else came in. They weren't fed. No bathroom visits. No nothing.

A few of the boys had slid down along the wall to sit on the floor. Every now and then, Cole or Gray would tell them to stand up in order to get the circulation back in their elevated hands. Gray stood stoically for the most part, just looking out one of the two small windows as the sun dipped lower and lower.

It was disappearing from the horizon when the engine started, causing a rush of nervousness to surge through the guys. Eyes more vigilant, muscles tensing up.

"Is this it?" Milo's eyes welled up. "Are we gonna be slaves?"

No one answered.

They shared a heavy silence for another couple hours until they reached a marina. Or they guessed it was a marina. Those who were closest to the windows could spot a handful of boats, and more than that, land. It made sense they docked at the edge of the marina, though. Easier to escape if it came to that.

"I can see the dock," Jackie said eagerly. "Can we scream for help?"

Gray doubted their voices would carry, but there was a way to test it out and stay somewhat safe. Fingers crossed. "We can ask if they're gonna give us food," he suggested. "If anyone out there hears us shouting, maybe we have a shot."

"Wait till you see someone who doesn't look like a guard," Cole told Jackie. "Then we'll try."

"Okay." Jackie nodded.

So they waited. Above them, they heard the clicking of heels and heavy footfalls of security. There was an air of anticipation that Gray feared. He hated not knowing how badly this was gonna go. The hell did he know of trafficking? Fucking squat. Should he expect people to die? How hurt was he gonna get? Was he gonna be taken to another country?

What was it going to take to make Gray agreeable to someone else? Nothing short of death and being permanently locked up in a dungeon would keep him in a place against his will.

That's not entirely true.

He flinched at the memory of what Bob had done to him. No, Gray had a limit. It wasn't just death that made him obey, and he hated himself for it.

"I only see those fucking guards." Jackie sounded like he was as close to tears as he was to a fit of rage.

The waiting was getting to them. Exhaustion, malnourishment, and thirst played a part, and the combination was breaking them down. One boy started crying, begging for his mom and dad to come get him. *I just want my mom, I just want my mom.* No one was unaffected because everyone could relate, and none of them did anything for the same reason.

At some point, there was more commotion above them. The guys exchanged glances, and at least Gray could count on Cole for sharing similar thoughts. The buyers had arrived. Midnight had been mentioned, hadn't it? Maybe that was the time they were set to arrive.

Faint sounds of laughter traveled below to their cabin. For shithead slave owners, this was a joyous occasion. It made Gray sick.

Only moments later, the yacht was moving again.

"There's no one on the dock." Jackie's eyes shone with panic. "Do we scream anyway?"

What was the point?

Gray swallowed hard. Every rumble of the engine, every little turn out of the marina...every yard farther away from land was a stitch in sealing their fate.

It was another couple of hours before the door opened and Red appeared with two goons, one of them the guard with a scar. She snapped her fingers and pointed at Charlie.

"Him first."

For reasons unknown to Gray, that was when he lost it. As Charlie began begging to be saved and swearing he'd do anything to go home, the fury in Gray was unleashed.

He turned his first glower at Red. "You fucking bitch, didn't your parents teach you to pick on kids your own size?"

"Please don't hurt me!" Charlie sobbed as a guard worked to unlock his restraints. "Please, please, please—nooo!"

"Hey! You steroid-pumped needle dick," Gray snapped at Scarface. "You've been dying to have a go with me. Come at me, motherfucker."

Red tittered a laugh, her voice too deep. "Don't fall for this, Benny."

Scarface—or *Benny*—was easily goaded, and he faced Gray with a dark grin that tugged at his scar. "You talk a lot, kid."

"I understand if the words are too difficult for you," Gray replied. "That's what happens when family members procreate." The mouth that had given him a lot of action on the ice in his years as a hockey player was about to give him a world of pain, but in this moment, he couldn't find it in him to care. Right this second, he had nothing to lose. "Is Daddy also Gramps?"

Cole piped in with a taunting chuckle and smirked at

Benny. "Is that it, dumbass? Are you one of those inbred sumbitches?"

Benny had already zeroed in on Gray, and as Red demanded her goon to stand his ground, he flew forward. Gray tensed up, and the last he heard was a cacophony of shouting and chains rustling. Then he inched back only to push forward and ram his forehead against Benny's nose. The force was enough to send the guard flying back, and Cole was quick to kick Benny in the ribs. Jackie followed, then another kid, and Gray drew in a deep breath through his nose. Adrenaline pumped freely, making it easy to ignore the pain in his head.

"What the hell are you just standing there for, ya fat fuck?" Gray shouted at the other guard. "Don't tell me they only hire slow mama's boys around here—"

"That's enough!" Red's voice became startlingly shrill when she shrieked. Next, she revealed a thin handle in her hand that ejected and became a cane. A torture device.

Yet, Gray pushed it. Hysteria bubbled up, his pulse skyrocketed, and he spat at her as he struggled fruitlessly against his shackles. "You're next, you ugly fucking hag. Don't think for a second I would hesitate to get my hands around your neck and snuff you out like a motherfucking candle."

The illusion of control and conviction belonged to him and the other boys for about ten seconds. It lifted their spirits and made them mentally stronger. Unfortunately, it made the fall more severe. Because when the cabin flooded with four other guards, everything came crashing down. Red whacked the silver cane squarely across Gray's face, then three times rapidly along his back as he hunched over. The screaming and cursing were drowned out by henchmen who took pleasure in silencing the guys.

Sharp pain shot through Gray, and blood trickled from his split eyebrow.

Red took a step closer and grabbed a fistful of Gray's hair. "This is why I lowered your price. Rebellious little fools are worthless." Her painted claws dug into his jaw. "I think we'll have to make an example out of you and offer you up as entertainment tonight." With that said, she pushed him away and stalked out.

Benny was next in line. His nose was broken, if not crushed, and he grabbed Gray's head before he slammed up his knee. Acting on instinct, Gray managed to tilt his face to save his nose, and the solid kneecap hit his cheek instead.

After that, he was a heap on the floor. More pain surged through him as he landed, effectively dislocating his shoulder because his hands were still fastened tightly to the wall.

His body screamed in protest, and he screwed his eyes shut so he didn't see when they dragged Charlie out of the cabin.

I'm sorry.

They were saving Gray for last.

With each guy they hauled out of the room, he grew more despondent and withdrawn. He'd managed to get on his feet again, but he could barely move without an explosion of hurt unfurling inside him. So he stood silent, face impassive and smeared with blood, eyes unseeing, as another guy was up.

The worst part was when they screamed wherever they were. Gray guessed a deck or two above him.

Were they getting raped yet?

He knew it was coming.

He stiffened as the door opened once more, and this time, it was Cole's turn. His features were set; he'd braced himself for whatever was to come. Or so Gray hoped. He couldn't imagine any of them had a clue what they were in for.

Least of all Gray. Were they gonna kill him? He'd watched enough movies to know what "make an example of someone" usually meant.

Milo was next, and he looked pleadingly at Gray. "Please do something," he whimpered. "I've never—I can't—please, Gray. P-please!"

Gray clenched his jaw and said nothing, because what the *fuck* could he do? The door was shut, leaving him alone. He listened. He couldn't *not* listen. Compelled and beating himself up, he strained his ears to hear every torturous plea.

It was quiet for some time, and then...then the screaming began. It mingled with muffled sobs and sharp, choking sounds. And low rumbles of laughter. There was even applause. Gray's stomach revolted and tightened. Nausea crept higher and higher. Milo was being abused, and low-life perverts found that funny.

The world became a dark place for Gray. Hope had dwindled enough that he couldn't see it anymore. He lost faith in humanity and sent a glance skyward as his eyes welled up. *Mom, I love you. Gage, Gideon, Gabriel, Aiden, Isla, the little niece or nephew I never got to meet...I love you, and I'm sorry.*

When the door was opened a final time, Gray was resigned. Benny stood there with sinister glee in his eyes, and of course, the brute wanted his fun, too. Gray accepted two fists to his face before he fell back against the wall, pain spreading like wildfire. Memories from better times that had been rolling past slowly gained speed as if he somehow knew time was running out.

Two men had to support Gray's weight on the way out of the cabin. His head hung, flickers of memories battling against fatigue and hurt. He couldn't see where they were going, and when they encountered a set of stairs, he stumbled and lurched. He focused on the faces of his family. Mostly, Mom and his three brothers. The recent additions were his stepdad—Aiden—

his daughter Isla, and Isla's fiancé, Jack. Gray loved the expansion of their family. The day he'd learned Isla was pregnant, he'd been so fucking thrilled. Now he'd never get to spoil his niece or nephew.

Something warm trickled down his face. He didn't know if it was blood or tears. Maybe a combination of both.

Gray was shoved into a large room, and the first glance with blurry vision made it look empty. Then he blinked and noticed there were booths along the far wall. The lighting was poor and focused on the middle, shadows cast everywhere. And he didn't care anymore. He gave up registering things.

"Your toy, sir," Benny said gruffly.

Vanya approached from the sidelines with a playful little smile, and the meatheads dropped Gray in the middle of the floor. He swallowed hard, his bleary gaze getting stuck on spots of red on the gray carpet. Once he saw a couple splatters, he noticed more. They were all over the center of the floor. Blood, then blotches of darker gray—maybe tears, sweat. *Semen*. The room reeked of it. A long silk robe came into view, the red fabric dancing around Vanya's feet. He squatted next to Gray and patted his head.

"There, there." Vanya's voice was still angelic and impossibly sweet. "Maybe we'll get to play more in another life. Mother said you're a bit of a moron."

Jesus, he was deranged.

Red sauntered closer, her thin metal cane ready to be used if needed. She didn't treat Gray as gently. Fisting his hair, she yanked him up on his knees, to which he hissed through clenched teeth.

They faced the darkened booths.

"Dear guests," Red purred, "I value my customers more than anything, and I would never lie to you." She slid the cane under Gray's chin, lifting it slightly. "This young man is more trouble than he's worth. Should you make a bid, you need to know you'll be getting a mouthy, rebellious hellion." With a sharp rap of the cane against his stomach, she ordered Gray to stand up.

He did so on wobbly legs. He'd reached his limit for torture for the moment and didn't want another bruise to his name.

"If there are no buyers on this animal," Red continued, "I'll offer him up as a treat for anyone and everyone—provided that you don't take him to your staterooms. He'll be available here in the central den throughout our journey." She paused. "Now. Let's see if there are any takers first. Starting at two hundred thousand, this wild boy could be yours. He's got gorgeous skin that scars nicely, doesn't he?" She shifted the cane along Gray's torso, and he swallowed against the vomit that rose. "As you can see on the menu, he is twenty-one years old and built for hot, sadistic grapples. He's six feet tall, weighs in at one hundred and eighty-nine pounds, and has the temper of an Irishman. If you keep him chained, he could bring you immense pleasure for years."

Gray steadied his breathing. Aside from a few barely there sounds of rustling and a throat clearing here and there, he wouldn't know there were people sitting in the booths.

"Lovely abs..." The whisper came from Vanya. Gray had almost forgotten him. Then the psycho kid from hell was tracing the muscles on his lower stomach. "My last toy called them come gutters." He giggled in delight.

Gray shuddered.

Someone coughed. "Two hundred." That *someone* was British and had a meek voice.

"Ah, we have a bidder." Red sounded both surprised and pleased. "Two hundred—"

"Two-fifty."

Gray swung his tired gaze to the corner, the first booth

there, and tried to see who it was. That man's voice was like low thunder doused in whiskey.

"Two hundred and seventy-five," the Brit said impatiently.

"Three hundred."

"Well, well," Red purred. "Three hundred for the handsome Mr. B."

The British man got irritated. "Three hundred and twenty."

"Three-fifty."

Silence.

Red ordered Gray to kneel again, and he merely dropped.

There was an insufferable huff coming from the booth where Gray believed the British man sat, but nothing else.

Gray didn't know what to think. This was his life. His freedom. Yet, two men were bidding on it. It was incomprehensible.

"Going once," Red said in a teasing tone. After a pause, it was made clear. "Mr. B, the heathen is yours. We hope to enjoy your show."

Oh fuck. Gray connected the dots. The auction was through, and once his life was no longer his own... It'd happened to the other guys. Eventually, he'd heard most of them scream in terror and agony.

A large man stepped out of the shadows in a swirl of his own cigarette smoke. Gray's eyes flicked between his briefcase, bespoke suit, and cut jaw. The rest was hazy. He couldn't focus. A headache was beginning to pull him under, and it was gonna be a big one. Mr. B didn't speak. Under the low light, his brown hair took on a lighter shade.

A stool appeared, delivered by a goon who quickly backed off. The man who now supposedly owned Gray set his briefcase on the stool and flicked open the lid.

Red and Vanya backed away, too.

Gray had lost all his strength. He remained kneeling on the floor and averted his gaze. This was it.

Mr. B approached and stood before a defeated Gray. There was a grip on his jaw, and Gray was forced to look up. His double vision prevented him from registering anything other than a set of hazel eyes brimming with severity and determination. He swallowed weakly as the man dipped and leaned in close. There was a whisper in Gray's ear.

"Forgive me."

A heartbeat later, Gray took a hard blow to the temple that shot his head sideways and knocked him out.

03

Gray didn't dare move a single muscle. He'd woken up in a big bed with his hands bound to a hook in the bedpost closest to his head. Someone had reset his shoulder after it was dislocated. Blood and tears stained the pillow, tears that continuously streamed down his cheeks. He hurt *everywhere*, and that included his ass. The man—this motherfucker they called Mr. B—had knocked him out and raped him.

Said man was in the stateroom right this second, one of the reasons Gray kept quiet and still. He had his back to Mr. B, who sat at the desk that faced the window. There was a mirror on the door to the bathroom that let Gray see what was going on behind him, and he couldn't look away from Mr. B's broad back. And the daylight. The tears were oddly soothing, like balm or aloe, and allowed him to stare directly at the blue sky without his eyes burning. Or perhaps his eyes had gotten adjusted to the light again.

He wasn't ready for the terror to continue. Judging by the number of scars that graced Mr. B's back, he was into some dangerous shit. If Gray didn't know better, he'd say the man had been flogged or whipped to the point where his skin had cracked. The long slashes were long since healed but had once been deep cuts. One scar on his shoulder looked like it could be from a gunshot wound.

"There are painkillers here." The man speaking up sent a jolt of shock through Gray, and he tensed up. "I'm guessing you're hurting."

"Fuck you." Gray's mouth got the best of him, and he instantly regretted it.

Idiot!

With no sudden movements, Mr. B rose from his chair and rounded the bed. Gray refused to face him, instead waiting for the punishment he'd get for insulting his *owner*. God, he wanted to die. He no longer saw a way out of this unless it involved a body bag and a tag on his toe.

Mr. B was only wearing a pair of dress pants, and from one of the pockets, he produced a switchblade that he ejected from its sheath.

Gray, having nothing left to lose, kept his stare trained at the mirror, though he could see the man's movements in his periphery. "Did you bring a knife to a gunfight?"

"I was unaware you had a gun."

Of course he didn't have a fucking gun. "Red pointed out to me that maybe a shooter would be interested in me."

"Red...? Ah, you mean Valerie." Mr. B walked closer and sat down on the edge of the bed, and Gray fought the urge to scoot back. "Shooters are heroin users. As in, shooting up. In this industry, they're known for keeping their slaves drugged."

"Okay." Gray waited for anger to rise at the use of *slaves*. Mr. B had said the word casually. Like they were discussing a game or the damn weather. But the anger didn't hit. Perhaps he really had surrendered and accepted his fate.

Heroin didn't sound half bad, though, a thought that resonated loudly as Mr. B dragged the sharp point of his blade along Gray's hip. Bad time to realize he wasn't wearing anything but a sheet that was riding low.

"Do I have your attention?"

Gray jerked a small nod and closed his eyes.

"Good. Now, look at me."

He didn't want to, but his free will didn't matter anymore, did it? He squeezed his eyes shut hard, then opened them slowly as two tears rolled down onto the pillow. Next, he slid his wary gaze to the man, seeing him in broad daylight for the first time. He remembered the hazel eyes. They were accompanied by faint crow's-feet at the corners. A five o'clock-shadow dusted his jaw. His expression was grim, and he looked to be in his early forties.

Gray furrowed his brow, a niggling sensation trying to jog a memory. He had *seen* this motherfucker before. Back home. He was almost sure of it. He just couldn't pinpoint when and where. Christ, was this how the slave traders knew who to kidnap? Had this man stalked him, maybe even talked to him, then decided to buy Gray?

"You recognize me," Mr. B stated.

Gray didn't reply.

For whatever reason, that made the asshole's mouth twist up a fraction. Then he stood up and grabbed a chair, dragging it over to sit down by the bed. Elbows resting on his knees, he did absent tricks with the blade and stared at Gray, as if he was thinking of what to say. Gray found himself staring at the knife.

He had no doubt the man could use it well. His stocky, yet sculpted chest bore other scars. One that matched the one on his shoulder, making Gray wonder if the bullet had gone straight through. Under his left pec, chest hair didn't grow because of a four-inch line that'd been stitched poorly at some point. His other pec was covered in a tattoo that traveled up to his shoulder and across his bicep. Despite being less than five feet away, Gray couldn't make out the details of the ink.

"I'm gonna have to hurt you if you freak out." Mr. B kept his voice low and his stare grave. "Can you listen to what I have to say without losing your temper, Gray?"

Gray opened his mouth to mutter a *sure*, only to snap it shut. *He used my name.* They probably had his name in his file, but it felt...*off*. Nobody used his name. His identity didn't matter to these people.

"There are cameras in this cabin." Mr. B gave him a pointed look. "There's no audio, but Valerie and her crew can see everything we do."

"Okay." It meant nothing to Gray.

Mr. B flipped out the blade again and wagged it lightly at Gray. "If you're wondering if I've fucked you up the ass, the answer is no. If you believe I own you, that answer is also no."

What the fuck was up with this moron? The soreness in Gray's ass sure as hell wasn't imaginary. "Whatever you say." He gave a flat look.

To which the motherfucker sighed. "All right. Listen, knucklehead. Your pop gave me unlimited funds to track you down and bring you home."

Gray merely smirked. Was the man trying to mess with his head? "Uh-huh."

A crease appeared in Mr. B's forehead. "You don't believe me?"

"Given that I don't have a dad, no." *Do your research better next time, jackass.*

The man narrowed his eyes. "Aiden Roe."

Okay, that did the trick. Aiden hadn't been part of the family that long, so it was still an adjustment. Though to an outsider, of course he was Gray's dad. He'd certainly shouldered the role better than anyone else.

"My stepdad," Gray rasped. His heartbeat drummed faster and faster as hope flared to life. Did this mean he was gonna see his family—wait. Just like that, hope could crash and burn too.

Someone who'd tailed him to gather information would know about Aiden.

"Semantics." Mr. B furrowed his brow. "I have a message from your mother that's supposed to help. Just remember to calm your tits. I really don't wanna slice you open." He paused and looked at Gray intently. "Under the old chair in the break room at the bed-and-breakfast, there's something that you and your ma keep hidden."

Gray blanched at that. He immediately knew what the man meant—and what it referred to. It was such a silly fucking secret. And such an emotional roller coaster it took him on now. He could feel hysteria claiming him again, and there was no holding back the hope anymore.

"Do you mean it?" he choked out.

"It's what your mother said."

Oh God. Could it really be...?

"You have to cut me," Gray gritted. Because a slap wouldn't make him cry. A mere discussion wouldn't move him to tears either. Mr. B was gonna have to give it to him good for the cameras.

Sensing the imminent breakdown, Mr. B cursed and stood up. Then he towered over Gray and held him in a light choke hold.

"Do you really mean it?" Gray croaked. "Am I gonna survive this?"

"Yeah. You are." Next, he pushed the blade against the fleshy part of Gray's thigh. The man knew exactly where to cut to make it look worse than it was, and as the blood began seeping freely, Gray let go. A low sob broke free, then another, and another. His hands were tied, so he hid his face against his shoulder, and he cried like a fucking baby.

Months of panic, anguish, hunger, nausea, thirst, deprivation, pain, and fear rolled off of him in heavy waves.

He truly hadn't believed he was ever gonna see his family again.

Part of him still didn't. He was just so desperate he'd cling to anything.

Please make it true.

"You need to at least pretend to struggle, Gray," Mr. B said quietly. "You ain't the type to just take it."

Gray whimpered, fresh tears rolling down, and offered a lame attempt to fight for his life.

Even with the pain of the new wound—and all the old ones—a big grin threatened to break free. Maybe he'd lost his mind. He didn't know. He didn't care.

Mr. B did. "Don't you fucking dare. Hold yourself together. They could be watching every goddamn move."

Gray couldn't help it. The frenzy of joy that surged in his veins unleashed a crazy little laugh, and he smiled even as he cried.

"For chrissakes." The man had reached his limit. Pocketing the knife, he smacked Gray's bloody thigh—hard—and then backhanded him across the face.

It was enough pain to override the relief.

"Ow!" Gray let out a hoarse cry and turned his face into the pillow.

Okay, I'll be good.

A trip to the bathroom gave Gray a bit of clarity, not to mention time for countless questions to pile up. The stateroom and its bathroom were lavish and screamed of wealth, with the exception of certain details whispering of cruelty and terror. Like hooks in the walls and furniture. One of his hands was cuffed to a metal hook above the toilet paper dispenser, and he had to let the man know when he was done.

"You can come in," he said as he yanked up his underwear and flushed the toilet. His black boxer briefs were loose on him, and they belonged to the other guy. They were brand-new. Still had the creases from being folded in the packaging.

Mr. B entered, and Gray went from being cuffed to one hook to another, this one above the sink. He really went all out not to raise any suspicion.

"Are there any cameras in here?"

"Above the mirror." Mr. B leaned against the doorway, having put on a white button-down, though it was unbuttoned. A black tie hung around his neck too. "You're dizzy."

Gray lifted a shoulder, then cupped his free hand under the pouring water and splashed some on his face. "I can't remember the last time I ate."

"I'll call for lunch. It'll be a while before we get outta here, so we need to talk. And you need to look like you hate being here."

Gray nodded once. "Sorry about before." It bothered him that he had no control of his emotions.

"No worries." Mr. B jerked his chin at the bedroom. "We'll talk while I dress your wounds. They can't blame a guy for wanting his property in good condition for more torture."

There was no stopping the shudder for Gray. He let the guy lead him to the bed where he was restrained once more, and he sat back against the headboard. First, Mr. B dialed room service, like this was some swanky hotel, and next, he grabbed a briefcase that revealed medical supplies.

Gray remembered a briefcase from last night too.

Three of them were stacked on the desk.

"What happened last night after you knocked me out?"

Mr. B's features tightened, and he focused on cleaning the long cut along Gray's thigh. It stung, though it was nothing in comparison. "They expected a show, so I had no choice but to give them one." He cleared his throat and flicked his gaze toward the briefcases. "I'm impersonating one of those shooters, by the way. I have enough heroin and other drugs to kill a horse over there."

Gray wasn't too surprised, mainly because he'd been out a long time. It didn't matter how skilled Mr. B was in combat; a punch didn't keep someone down for that many hours. He must've injected Gray with something.

"It was the most humane way I could think of. Whatever I did to you, you would have no recollection of."

"My ass does hurt, you know." A bit of anger and shame colored Gray's cheeks.

Mr. B inclined his head and wiped away the last of the blood. "I sized you out for toys and marked you."

Gray averted his eyes instantly. It seemed anxiety and a bunch of other useless emotions were never far away. What he'd learned now was a punch in the gut, and he was embarrassed. Embarrassed, angry, and hurt.

"How did you mark me?" His voice grew low and dull, and he stared at his lap.

"They tattooed a barcode on the back of your neck," he said. "To showcase my ownership, I carved in numbers below it."

Carved.

"I don't feel it," Gray whispered. This clusterfuck was getting to be too much again—too overwhelming. Maybe this guy would free him. Maybe he'd get to return to his family, but he carried doubts about whether or not his body was still his. He'd never felt so violated.

He didn't necessarily blame Mr. B for that. Just...this whole mess.

"You will." Mr. B bit off a strip of surgical tape and finished dressing the wound. "The lidocaine wears off pretty quickly. Eventually, so does shock."

What else had he been up to while Gray was dead to the world?

"Are you really here to save me?" He needed reassurance.

"Yes, Gray."

"How can I be sure?"

The man flashed an ounce of sympathy, though that was it. However, Gray could hear it in his voice when he spoke. "If the message from your mother wasn't enough…" Mr. B eased off the bed and used the chair instead, where he retrieved a crumpled pack of smokes and lit one up. "You've probably seen me around." He blew some smoke toward the ceiling. "Like most other kids involved in sports in our town, I'm guessing you go to the gym down on Hemlock." So he was a local? He was from Camassia too? "That's my little brother's gym. Ethan Quinn. According to my research, you went to private school, and seeing as Camassia only has one, I'mma venture a guess and say you've heard of Avery Becker." Well, yeah. Social studies teacher at Ponderosa High. "He's one of my closest friends."

Gray stared at him and didn't say a word. He also grew more conscious of the cameras, for once, and he did his best to look angry and broken and miserable and not at all hopeful and wistful.

"My youngest sister," Mr. B went on, "beat you and your family last summer at the festival's apple contest. Elise's popsicles against your mother's apple cider and pies. If I remember correctly, your twin brothers got pissy."

Gray pressed his lips together in a tight line, even though he wanted to cry from sheer happiness again. Hearing these inconsequential—in the grand scheme of things—little anecdotes brought forth enough memories that he could practically smell the forest from back home. He could taste the sea in the air, hear

Gabriel and Gid bitching about that woman's popsicles, which was promptly followed by Mom chastising them and lecturing them about sportsmanship. Afterward, Mom, Aiden, Isla, and Gray had bought some popsicles from Elise's stand.

They'd been awesome.

Gray took a wild guess and assumed Mr. B had nothing whatsoever to do with his real name.

"You've probably been to my restaurant in the marina too," he said. "But most of all, I know Madigan and Abel." Holy shit. Gray's heart thumped wildly at the mention of his best friend and his fiancé. "It was Madigan who asked me for help and introduced me to your folks." He leaned back and buttoned his shirt, one of his feet coming up to rest on the edge of the bed. "Anyway. I'm Darius Quinn. Keep that name out of your mouth while we're here."

Gray's eyes welled up, and he swallowed around the lump in his throat. "Thank you."

"Your dad pays well."

Oh, so that's how it was gonna be. Fair enough. "Do I wanna know how much I'm worth?"

The left corner of Darius's mouth turned up. "That answer will always depend on who you're asking."

"I'm not worth much to slave traders," he pointed out. "What did I go for, three hundred and fifty thousand?" Everything that happened last night was fuzzy at best.

Darius nodded once. "We like to think we're worth more than we are. These types of auctions...they're more rare. Wealthy men who lead secret lives have specific requests and tastes. I can get an orphan for a few bucks in Cambodia, a ladyboy in Thailand for a couple grand..." He started tying his tie with practiced ease. "Right here in the Land of the Free, I can get a domestic girl for twenty thousand."

"You're not serious." Gray was fucking horrified—or he would be, if he could get a grasp on his emotions.

"As a heart attack." Darius rose from his chair and grabbed his polished shoes. "Human trafficking is as common as STDs, Gray. At the risk of crushin' your ego, you were expensive because the organization had a dozen buyers who specifically wanted young gay men with athletic builds, Caucasian looks, and wholesome backgrounds. There was a demand, so the supply got pricey. You're a secret trophy, nothing else."

Gray felt like the world he knew was an illusion.

"You think that's bad?" Darius drawled. "A big percentage of the sellers who offer up kids for a quick buck are their parents."

Gray couldn't even fathom that. It didn't compute.

"Why the wholesome backgrounds?" Another thing that didn't make any sense.

"A happy kid isn't as equipped to deal when everything gets taken away from him."

Jesus Christ. Gray could only shake his head. It was surreal how evil people could be. Taking someone's freedom wasn't enough. They had to twist the knife even more and find other ways to add to the suffering.

Darius didn't seem bothered by it. "Sometimes, there's a demand for the opposite. You can't expect to use rhyme or reason with these people."

"How come you know so much about it?" Gray eyed him dubiously. "You said you own a restaurant, and now you're here..."

"I wasn't always a restaurant owner." Darius left it at that, and then there was a knock on the door.

Lunch had arrived.

04

"I'm sorry, kid."

Gray shook his head, unsure of whether he cared or not. What he didn't want, however, was a meaningless apology from Darius.

To keep up appearances, Gray had to suffer a lot—and often—not to raise any suspicion from those who might be watching them in their cabin. For lunch, Darius had decided the suffering included degradation. So Gray sat on the floor, his back to the bathroom door, one hand cuffed to another goddamn hook in the wall, and ate from a bowl reserved for dogs.

"If physical pain hurts less, say the word," Darius said. He sat at his desk, though he'd turned his seat a bit in Gray's direction. "I'd rather take a beating than humiliation, but your body's been through a lot."

Sticks and stones and all that.

Gray was undecided there, too. He almost blurted out, *But at least you haven't actually shoved your cock up my ass against my will*. Which was proof of how much his mind had sunk already. A part of him questioned his self-worth, and he viewed not getting raped as a thing to be thankful for. It was like thanking a bully for not being overly cruel one day.

"I don't envy you," Gray settled for mumbling. He wouldn't be able to inflict this sort of torture.

He picked at the food with his fingers. It was good—steak, fries, and sauce—and he ate it slowly. He remembered once after hockey camp, he'd come home and gorged on sugar and fat. Going from a diet of slow carbs and protein, it was no wonder he'd spent the next two days cramping like he was having a never-ending seizure. This time, he was going from a packet of rice and steamed vegetables a day to...steak. The fries were admittedly delicious.

His hunger came and went with each bite. His body *had* been through too much.

He shifted, the new angle giving him an uncomfortable reminder of what Darius had been forced to do to Gray last night. He didn't wanna think about it. It was fucking embarrassing.

"So when are we getting out of here?" he asked. The sooner, the better. "I just wanna get back to normal." And the second they got the chance, they had to call the police—hell, bring in the National Guard for all he cared. Whatever they did, they had to time it so the other guys didn't suffer because Gray got free.

"There is no going back to normal." Darius wiped his mouth with an expensive napkin and pushed away his plate. Then he turned the chair farther, putting his legs up on the bed, and reached for his smokes. "Once we get out, all this will hit you more than it already has. You're in survival mode now. I bet some of the shit you've been through doesn't even faze you at the moment."

Gray licked sauce off his thumb and eyed Darius warily. "Your bedside manner leaves a lot to be desired, you know."

He lit up a cigarette. "Good thing I'm no doctor. As for when we get out of here...about three days from now. Give or take."

"*That* long?" What the fuck! Couldn't they just— He

stopped short, unable to finish that sentence. Couldn't they just *what*? Swim to shore? Gray had no clue of their whereabouts and how long they planned on being out at sea. "Um. What's the plan? Are we headed someplace?"

"Joulter Cays," Darius confirmed. That name rang a bell. *Joulter*. "Seven of us completed transactions last night. The other buyers were escorted to another auction, and the rest of us learned our destination." He had a map splayed out on the desk, though he didn't offer it to Gray. "Boats will be waiting there to take us wherever we wanna go."

"There were eight of us," Gray was quick to point out.

"Someone bought two boys."

Sick sons of bitches. Gray would never understand that level of depravity.

"So that's it?" It seemed too easy. "We'll go to this Joulter Cays place, and a boat will take us to the closest city where we take a flight home?"

"Well, we're gonna report in at the closest police station first, but yeah."

Gray chewed on his thumbnail. The plan didn't sit right with him at all. "We won't know where the other guys are going once we split up. They can be taken to fuckin' Russia or something."

"I wasn't sent here to rescue them."

Gray's eyes flashed to Darius's, and anger flared up.

Darius held the stare with what was becoming his standard expression. Impassive, matter-of-fact. "You don't accept one mission and go on another."

"Christ. Don't you have a fucking heart?" Gray blurted. That earned him a reaction. Darius's mouth flattened coldly. Gray wasn't done. "There's gotta be something we can do. I'm not some damsel in distress, man. I can help out. *We* can help."

It surprised him how much this mattered to him, but after

spending so much time with the other seven guys—two of them literally still children—Gray couldn't in good conscience just walk. He was probably naïve as hell; it made no difference. There had to be a way they could all get off this boat.

Darius took a slow drag from his smoke and rose momentarily to open a vent next to the window. "Do you know their final method for ensuring no buyers are cops or Feds? Other than weeks—sometimes months—of vetting." It was a rhetorical question, so Gray waited for the answer. "They spend time with us on board. They host the auctions at sea and expect to see our participation for days, and no agency in the US would send an undercover agent to repeatedly rape and abuse a victim. This—what I'm doing to you?" He twirled a finger between them. "It's nothing but sexual abuse. To get you outta here, I gotta put you through hell."

"Okay." Gray grew frustrated. He didn't care about semantics. He could take a few beatings, and he'd wager that the other boys would agree—if it meant they could walk away in the end. "Beats the alternative."

"One thing less shitty than another doesn't make it legal, and even our authorities have limits for what they can permit. This is about more than fucking whores and making bones," he said. "You're missing the point, though. We have three more days on this boat, and we haven't even left the stateroom yet. Get through those before you think about playing hero."

Although Gray was sure he wouldn't change his mind about wanting to help the others, he took a step back from the argument because there were still a lot of questions he wanted answered.

"How did you become a buyer? Were you vetted for weeks?" He dipped his fingers into his food again and dared another piece of steak. "How did you get involved at all?"

Darius inhaled from his cigarette again, eyes slightly

narrowed. It looked like he was deciding what was okay to share. "I'd already been vetted. The Feds arrested a buyer, and I borrowed his identity."

That didn't seem safe at all to Gray. "Are you sure he won't speak? Is he still in custody? How did the organization not know his face?"

That was too many questions for Darius, who picked only one to answer. "Money offers more loyalty than facial recognition, and privacy is everything to these buyers." He paused. "The sector that does the vetting meets with everyone, but no paper trail or exchange of IDs is involved. They wouldn't have any buyers if they required that." Reaching for something on the desk, he picked up a little black device, no bigger than a box of matches. "Once you're in, you get one of these. It'll send a signal when they've found what you're looking for, and it becomes your ticket to board."

So somewhere, that device had gone off when Gray had been kidnapped. Someone had put down preferences Gray matched with.

He was no longer hungry.

"If the Feds arrested him and already had this info—"

"They didn't. They had the buyer but nothing else."

In other words, Darius had pieced together the rest on his own. How, Gray didn't have the slightest idea.

"If you figured out so much, why didn't you tell the Feds?"

At that, Darius actually cracked a smile. "The fuck're they gonna do about it besides file paperwork for an eternity and orchestrate a half-assed rescue op?" He shook his head. "I have respect for federal agents, but they're buried. A missing person from Washington isn't a priority—not with the odds stacked against them. It's almost impossible to take down the higher-ups in these networks."

"Like Red?" Gray tilted his head. "She's right here! They can swoop in and take her."

Darius chuckled and put out his smoke. "She's a replaceable no-name cunt." He cleared his throat. "Listen. I know you got questions coming outta every orifice, but we gotta set boundaries. We have dinner tonight with the others, meaning we have to put on a show. Planning that takes precedence over satisfying your curiosity." The look in his eyes was serious enough that Gray bit back a response that would've come out too sarcastic anyway. "In short, I gotta know what you're okay with in terms of violence and sexual activities."

Okay was relative as fuck.

As much as it made Gray's stomach churn, he couldn't avoid the topic. Three days, that was how long they'd be on this yacht. Three days of ensuring that Red and the others believed Gray was Darius's property.

"I can handle violence." Gray lowered his gaze. "Sex too, I guess." Fuck, he felt dirty through and through. Another time and place, he probably would've jumped Darius at the first chance. He looked exactly like Gray's type, and it wasn't as if things were going anywhere with Craig, who, right now, existed in another world. Besides, Gray's heart and body didn't speak the same language.

"I'll make it as easy for you as I can," Darius said. "I brought Viagra—"

Gray's head shot up. "What?"

"I gotta look like I enjoy it," Darius pointed out.

Yeah, even under these circumstances, Gray managed to feel insulted. He didn't *want* to get down on his knees and suck this bastard's dick, but he wasn't gonna be rude.

"You're straight, I get it," he replied tightly. He bristled when Darius let out a chuckle.

"You're a good-looking kid, and no offense, you shouldn't—"

"None taken," Gray answered, more annoyed than he should be. "Gee, I wonder why Abel and Madigan never introduced me to you. You're such a nice man."

That wiped the smirk off Darius's face. "Your arrogance is less desirable. You also look fucking stupid when you make assumptions. Even if you had tits, I would've needed help. Because unlike the motherfuckers on this boat, I actually don't get off on hurting my partners."

Oh. Well, didn't Gray just feel dumb as fuck now.

He looked away and chewed on the inside of his cheek.

"If you're done with your tantrum, let's talk about dinner," Darius said.

Leaving the stateroom that evening caused Gray's heart to plummet. For a precious day, he'd gotten a break from uncertainty and vicious abuse. Darius had made him believe they were heading home after this, and he still believed. He did. But first, he had to pretend, and there was no room for error whatsoever.

The yacht seemed even more luxurious tonight. His eyes weren't swollen shut, his body was recovering, and he wasn't being dragged toward his own auction.

One.

As instructed, he walked behind Darius, eyes downcast, and he counted every person he saw. To get a better estimate of just how many people were on board.

Two, three, four.

Dinner was held on the top deck, which was completely open and offered a 360-degree view of a stunning sunset. A pool took up most of the front. Closer to the middle, where they'd come up, was an elevated sundeck.

There had to be at least twenty people up here, and Gray gave up on counting for now. Men—and a couple women—were dressed to the nines and enjoying themselves with champagne and fancy snacks that four young guys were delivering on serving trays. They didn't look like ordinary waitstaff, though. Dressed much like Gray, in underwear and nothing else, they looked every bit a slave as he did.

A table for twelve was set under a canvas ceiling along the aft deck, and Gray scanned the guests discreetly in hopes of seeing…could he call them friends? Fellow victims. The innocent guys in a sea of monsters.

Darius was greeted by some of the other shitheads, most of them complimenting the "lovely marks" on Gray. Overnight, his bruises had turned dark and blotchy.

Gray tuned it all out when he spotted four familiar faces. Cole, Charlie, Lee, and Milo were kneeling by the railing, and they were attached to four of the eleven or twelve metal posts. Their bodies were bruised and battered, and Milo's face broke Gray from within. The kid was shaking, tears running down his cheeks, and he could barely open his eyes.

"Can you buy Milo?" Gray spoke under his breath and had to repeat himself a couple times before Darius heard him. "Dar—Mr. B. Milo—can you buy him?"

Darius cleared his throat and glanced over at the boys. "He went for over two million. I don't think his owner's looking to part with him anytime soon."

Two million.

Jesus fucking Christ.

All because he looked like a child. He *was* a child. White-hot rage festered inside Gray and grew like a cancer. If Darius thought a few days of torture and forceful fucking were gonna change Gray's mind about helping the others, he was dead wrong. He wasn't getting off this yacht without the other guys.

"I'll see what I can do." Darius's final words offered a bit of comfort.

Gray fucking ached to get close enough to the guys so he could tell them they had a plan. But for one, Darius had forbidden him to. For two, there wasn't a plan that included them all. Yet.

The twelve who were seated included the buyers, two spouses, Red, Vanya, and one man Gray didn't recognize. Kneeling behind Darius's chair, Gray observed and listened. It was a dinner for pompous fuckwits to brag about their cruelty. The majority of them were Americans who'd taken up residence in other countries, mainly in South America and the Middle East.

During appetizers, the British man who'd wanted to buy Gray last night complained about his purchase. Whoever he'd bought didn't scream when having his fingers broken.

Gray wondered who he'd bought. Cole was the one who struck Gray as tough as nails.

When the main course was served, a man with a thick drawl invited them all to his estate in Belize.

"I've heard of your hunts, Mr. K," Red said, intrigued. "What was it last year, trap shooting?"

"My wife and I attended," another guy said. "We had great fun, indeed."

"That is correct, ma'am." There was pride in the Texan's voice. "We acquired six local boys, and they all got a turn in the cannon. Sometimes we miss—or we shoot them in the leg instead of the head. Most of them die upon impact with the ground, but if they don't, they get a second try."

While Gray had to swallow shock and bile, someone

clapped. *Vanya.* That disturbed little man. He looked positively gleeful.

What the fuck was wrong with people?

Throughout dinner, Gray heard gory tales that came straight from nightmares. A few of the buyers collected girls too, and each death was more horrifying than the last. Electrocution, forced overdose, drowning, being buried alive. Gray listened as one man told them about the time he threw two girls into a cage and said only one would get out alive. He'd had fucking dinner guests over to watch.

Gray swayed, a dizzy spell catching him. He didn't wanna live in a world where this was happening. They were laughing about medieval torture and making plans for future events.

"You haven't said a word, Mr. B," Red noted curiously.

Gray caught himself and took a deep breath. In this position, he could see Darius cutting into the last of his steak and putting it in his mouth. He appeared unfazed by the whole thing.

"Physical sadism never impressed me much. A mentally challenged toddler can inflict pain." He chewed slowly and wiped his mouth with the linen napkin. In the meantime, the others around him looked a little offended. "Violence is necessary sometimes, of course." Darius was cleaning up his speech, Gray noticed. "But there's a reason Mr. S here needs a choker made of barbed wire for his boy and I don't." Everyone's attention shifted to Gray, who went rigid and looked down.

"You've had him less than twenty-four hours," Vanya stated.

The Texan scoffed. "Of course he doesn't need restraints. You're a shooter. When we use rope and whatnot, you use heroin."

Another one piped up in agreement. "If anything, I always thought drug users were lazy."

"He's not on anything now." Darius sat back and sipped his wine. "Controlling his mind—that's the real challenge."

"Mental sadism always fascinated me." Red was eating up every word. "Do tell us your methods. I love a man who possesses that skill."

Gray clenched his jaw. What was Darius up to? There better be a good fucking answer.

"I gave him hope," Darius murmured. "You have to see his journey here as a tool. Most of you forget that—or neglect it, and it's a shame. He's had weeks of being pushed down mentally. When I bought him, he was already defeated." He paused to polish off the rest of his wine. "Unlike what many believe, you can gain strength from physical pain. *You* could, unknowingly, be giving your slaves stronger minds by beating them. But me? I want my property desperate and weak. That's when the real play begins."

Gray swallowed hard, queasy. Uncertainty flowed freely in his veins, and he began going through everything Darius had told him in the cabin.

"Incredible," Red said in awe. "Because when they're desperate and weak, they'll believe anything."

No. There was no way. Darius was just acting.

"How did you give him hope?" Vanya asked as the Texan said, "Now, I don't believe that. Not that they'll grow stronger from receiving pain."

"You first, Mr. K," Vanya allowed.

So Darius addressed the Texan first. "We're primitive creatures, my friend, but we live in an intelligent world. These boys were brought up to know the difference between good violence and bad, and the pain you're putting them through makes you no better than a schoolyard bully. They may end up on the ground by force, but they'll know you're mentally weak as shit. Pardon my French."

A low murmur traveled across the dinner table, some pondering the truths Darius had spoken, some in obvious disagreement.

Darius was too fucking good, in Gray's opinion. He was doubting himself and how quickly he'd believed Darius. *When we're desperate and weak, we'll believe anything.* It hit too close.

"I'm not mentally weak," the British guy scoffed.

Darius reached into his pocket and retrieved a cigar. "Don't tell *me* that. Tell your slave. But if you think he submits—if you think his mind collapses—when you beat him, think again. Your property wishes you dead."

The Texan seemed to be switching gears. "What you're sayin' is you want complete enslavement. You want power over their thoughts too."

Darius furrowed his brow. "Don't we all?"

Red tinkered a laugh and snapped her fingers for a guy to refill Darius's drink. "This calls for a toast. And where's dessert?"

Vanya wasn't finished, and he spoke up while the deck filled with waitstaff and two guys who lit candles everywhere now that the sun had set. "You must've promised quite hefty rewards to make your slave compliant so quickly."

"Oh, my dear son," Red said, "that one is fairly obvious. All he has to do is promise freedom."

The word smacked Gray in the face, and he flinched.

"Is that what you did, sir?" Vanya asked.

Darius inclined his head. "I did more than that. I made him believe I was here to rescue him."

All the air escaped Gray's lungs in a painful whoosh as if it'd been knocked out of him, and something inside of him shattered. *No. Please.* He wouldn't live through this. Close to hyperventilating, he tried to force himself to think clearly, but everything was a haze. He heard laughter at the table. It'd all been a game for Darius—*no*. It couldn't have been! Abel and Madigan had asked him for help! *Dumbass, he could've seen them on your Facebook and put two and two together.* Oh God. Maybe Gray was fairly private on Facebook, but he did have all his friends listed there. He wasn't a code to crack. All one had to do was pay attention for more than ten minutes.

He must've missed a question, because the next thing he knew, Darius was scooting back his chair and gripping Gray's jaw.

"This is why. Look at the boy's face." Darius tightened his hold, and Gray let out a whimpered breath. His eyes filled rapidly with tears, and the betrayal burned like lava. "He's crushed."

Gray glared murderously through the tears. "You sack of shit," he rasped. "You lied to me."

Darius chuckled and withdrew his hand, then spoke to the others while he pulled something from the inside of his suit jacket. "This can be done over and over, because they're clinging to hope, and you're all they've got."

Anger blazed through Gray, and he flew at Darius with his fists clenched. Unfortunately, everyone but Darius was shocked, and he swiftly grabbed Gray by his throat and hauled him to his feet. Gray choked and shoved at Darius, who pressed a sharp object to Gray's neck. *Oh shit. No!* A second later, a needle pierced his skin, and he was injected with something.

"I'll fucking end you!" Gray shouted hoarsely.

There was more laughter, and Red applauded. *Fucking cunt*. Gray's head swam in something thick and sluggish, and his tongue felt weird.

"When he wakes up, I'll start all over again." The smug satisfaction in Darius's voice made Gray angrier than he'd ever been. He hated the world, he hated these monsters, he hated everything. His heart hammered in his chest, and tears streamed down his cheeks. The rage exploded further as his fighting got weaker. He lost control of his limbs, his arms and legs prickling and going numb.

"Kill me," he sobbed. The defeat crushed him. It felt like his chest was about to cave in. His eyelids fluttered, and he sagged against Darius. "Just...k-kill me."

Everything went black.

05

"What the hell are you saying? You've been spying on us? That's a violation of my privacy."

Gray twitched and furrowed his brow, the words plucking at the cobwebs of sleep. *Something about spying...*

"I'm sorry, Mr. B, it's an insurance policy." That voice was unfamiliar. "To be absolutely positive the wrong guests don't get on board. I assure you, we haven't heard anything, but it's essential we get a glimpse of our esteemed guests' private routine."

The shuffling around the bed pulled Gray further away from sleep, and he shifted slightly—*ow*. The lingering aches and protesting joints were a painful reminder of everything that'd happened. *Darius betrayed me. He fucking drugged me. Again.* The memories from last night were hazy at best. He remembered waking up a few times in the middle of the night, disoriented, and he remembered sleepy murmurs—Darius's voice. Not what had been said.

What Gray did have a perfect recollection of was what a goddamn idiot he was.

He wasn't going home. He wasn't gonna see his family again.

"There. All gone. I'll get out of your way. Apologies again, sir."

The door clicked shut, and Gray stayed still. Between the

pulsing thuds of his headache, he heard Darius move around. There was a faint signal, the sound following him.

Gray wasn't attached to anything. His hands were free. Did he stand a chance if he fought his way out of the room? He did his best to keep his breathing even at the thought of getting away. They were on the third deck, near the bow, and if he wasn't mistaken, there was a staircase nearby. One floor separated him from the top deck where he could jump into the water.

That'd be the end of him, but he'd die free. Unless he could drift to a nearby island...? No, too good to be true. They were probably out on the open water, miles away from land. Still, the smallest opportunity—

"I know you're awake, knucklehead."

Gray stiffened, then lifted his head and glanced around him, bleary-eyed. Darius was running a thin device underneath the flat screen on the wall, so he had his back to Gray.

He blinked to clear his vision and was once again greeted by the scars that graced Darius's broad back. He was muscled as fuck in a subtle way. When standing still, there was little to no definition. Then he moved, and everything flexed under a layer of flesh.

It wasn't often Gray looked small next to someone else, not even now when he'd lost weight. Darius had to be at least six-four, and he was built for combat. Strong and ready to fight, yet lean enough to be a fast runner. Those extra few pounds could be from his years as a restaurant owner. Did that make him a retired soldier—ah, no. Because he was a fucking liar, and Gray had no idea if there even was a restaurant.

"Congrats, you fucked me over." Gray cleared his throat and winced as he sat up.

Darius didn't miss a beat. "Note that I haven't cuffed you. If you wanna try to take me down, now's your chance. But before you go there, remember everything I've said."

It was a little hard to do that when everything hurt. Thankfully, not his ass this time.

Darius set the device down and turned to face the bed, arms folded across his chest. He was only a few feet away from the door and would block it easily. "I didn't fuck you over, Gray. I improved our cover and probably spared your friends one night of rape and physical torture."

Gray's feet landed on the floor with a muted slap. The dark wood was so polished you could eat off of it. "I don't believe a goddamn word you say."

"That's your emotions speaking," Darius stated. "If you used your head, you'd come to another conclusion. You'd remember what I said about your mother, about my sister—"

"So what?" Gray snapped. He glared at the motherfucker. "Maybe you're from Camassia. Maybe that restaurant in the marina is really yours. Maybe you talked to my mom, but *so what*? It doesn't prove you're here to take me home."

"You're right." He dipped his chin. "I've been casing you since you were born. I infiltrated a town and brought my entire family into it—"

"Asshole," Gray growled. "That's not what I meant."

"I'm aware." Darius sighed and walked over to sit down next to Gray on the edge of the bed. "Listen. I didn't wanna take this job, but when shit falls into my lap, I can't ignore it for too long."

"I'm the shit?"

"You're the shit," he confirmed. "And if you want, this can be over and done with tonight. I return home, you return to your family."

Gray furrowed his brow at him, only to shake his head and look down again. "You're getting your lies mixed up. Yesterday, you said we had to wait three days."

"It's safer for your friends if we wait," Darius replied. "These are men who lash out at the wrong people when they get cornered or threatened. If they wake up tomorrow and you and I are gone, the boys will be the recipients of the owners' initial fear of getting caught—and anger."

Gray groaned inwardly and scrubbed at his face. He felt weak in every sense of the word and didn't know what to believe anymore. His head swam with hope and cynicism, constantly tugging him in different directions.

The worst hadn't been when his world had caved in. It was now, when he stood there in the rubble and didn't know if there was any way out of ground zero. One wrong move could cause everything to collapse further.

"I wanna believe you so fucking much," he whispered, staring unseeingly at his hands that'd fallen to his lap. He used to think of himself as strong.

"I know, kid. You've been dealt one fucked-up hand." Sympathy made an appearance in Darius's voice.

Gray side-eyed him, so confused it hurt, and tried to make sense of things. Where Darius was concerned, anyway. The man had been right. The dickbag slave traders on this boat were the only ones who could give the guys freedom, and Gray had no space for arrogance or pride. He recognized how easily Darius could play him again, yet Gray would probably keep coming back to the safe space of believing. Because what else could he do?

For several hours yesterday, he'd been granted hope and anxious relief. He wanted that again.

"What were you before you owned a restaurant?" he asked quietly, observing Darius with all the concentration he could punch through the exhaustion.

Darius didn't reply, and then he was saved by a knock on the door.

Breakfast had arrived, and the scar-faced Benny waited right outside the stateroom while a younger man set the trays of food on the desk by the window.

Gray stared at Benny, who smirked and leaned casually against the doorframe, a toothpick dangling from the corner of his mouth.

Hatred simmered below the surface, and Gray slowly white-knuckled the edge of the bed.

"Captivity suits you, sweethea—"

"Come here and I'll fuck you right up, sunshine," Gray cut in. "I've already done it once." He jerked his chin at the mother-fucker. "Nice nose job."

Benny's features darkened and tightened.

Darius took that moment to let the other man out, and he squeezed Benny's neck. To Gray, it looked like they were pals.

"You don't speak to my property." Darius spoke without an ounce of malice or threat, but there was *something*. "Remember, Benjamin, everyone has a price, and that includes you."

Benny straightened and cleared his throat, sparing Darius a quick glance that said he knew—and hated—he was beneath Darius on this boat, then walked away with the server.

Darius closed the door and walked over to the desk. "So you're the reason his nose looks like a purple golf ball." He started plating eggs, bacon, and toast. "No wonder Valerie said you're more trouble than you're worth."

Gray said nothing but sat a little straighter.

"Come here and eat," Darius told him. "It's time to build up your strength. I'm gonna need you if we're bringing the other boys with us."

That had Gray's attention. He instantly grew wary, fearing it was another trick, but he couldn't help going through the exact steps Darius had boasted about at dinner last night. At his weakest, Gray would believe anything. Here he was again.

"What changed your mind?" He shuffled around the bed and sat down in the chair Darius pulled out for him. There was another chair in the corner.

"Profiling," Darius muttered. "I'm gonna take a shot in the dark and say your backyard is full of dead animals you tried to rescue as a kid. Birds, rodents, the occasional rabbit."

A mouthful of scrambled eggs slid down Gray's throat with a portion of childish guilt. "No," he replied stubbornly. "Mom made me bury them in the woods."

Darius's mouth twitched, and he unwrapped his utensils. "Same shit. You've got a bleeding heart."

Profiling... Gray stared and stared as Darius tucked into his breakfast, and no conclusions came to him. All he saw was Darius's no doubt violent past, and he only saw it because of the scars on the man's body. Had he been a cop? Military? He didn't strike Gray as rigid and structured. A classmate's mom was in the army, and she carried herself a certain way.

Whatever Darius had been, he had the ability to profile Gray.

Darius noticed the staring and reached for his coffee with a sigh. "I was a PMC."

"PM, what?"

"Private military contractor."

Oh. Gray had heard of that and had even seen some recruitment videos online. They were the type of organizations that always lured in people with lines like, "We'll go where no one else will" and "When everything else fails, we're there."

"Isn't that for people with a death wish?" he asked hesitantly.

Darius chuckled under his breath and snatched up a piece of bacon. "I guess it can be. Just like the regular military, a lot of it gets amped up for publicity."

Oh really, because unless Gray was seeing things, Darius

was *here*. Right now. Not the safest mission, even though this wasn't one in that sense.

"Why the private sector?" Gray asked next. "Don't say money. I don't buy it."

He wasn't quite sure why he didn't buy it, only that it hadn't rung true whatsoever when Darius had made the comment about Aiden paying well to get Gray home.

"So now he's clearheaded." Darius spoke to himself. Gray scowled, having forgotten himself, and just like that, the doubts returned. What did he know about anything? "The private sector is easier. Less protocol to follow, which is why the military doesn't often like us. You get an order, and you follow through—often by any means necessary."

Less paperwork too, Gray guessed. He wasn't one of those who believed the government always followed the law, and contracting people like Darius probably made it easier to cover things up.

"So...are you a merc?"

Darius looked both amused and confused. "Don't use terms you don't understand."

"I know what a mercenary is. I saw a documentary about Blackwater."

"I'm sure it was very entertaining."

"People died."

"I remember." The tic in Darius's jaw as he refocused on his food made Gray think twice about pushing it. "It's not who I am anymore, so it doesn't matter. What matters is getting you and the others home." He nodded at Gray's plate. "Eat. You'll be pushed past your limits for this, and I can't afford to cut you any slack."

Hunger was something Gray had known since he started playing hockey. He had the appetite of a football team, yet today it was nowhere to be found. His energy levels were at an all-time low. Had yesterday been a fluke? His stomach had snarled for food, and it'd been delicious. Fuck, was his body growing accustomed to the malnourishment and shutting down? When was the last time he went to the bathroom?

It hit him what he was asking of Darius. Gray and the others had no fucking clue about much of anything, and they were physically and emotionally weakened. How the hell would they get out alive? He couldn't imagine the burden on Darius's shoulders.

"Are you really here to save me?" he asked once more.

"Yes, Gray."

Gray swallowed and forced himself to shovel more eggs into his mouth. In order to find the determination to be everything Darius needed for them to get out of here, he would have to believe and trust—again. Maybe he already did. At this point, everything looked bleak, and clinging to hope was dangerously easy.

"What made you change your mind about including the others?"

Darius took out a notepad from the desk drawer. "You. Short of being knocked unconscious, you won't leave the others behind."

That was true, and Gray couldn't feel bad about it. "Would you? You saw them at the auctions—and yesterday at dinner. Would you have been able to leave them?"

No answer.

The things Darius must've witnessed with his own eyes... It turned Gray's stomach.

"How many were raped?" Gray hated asking, and his voice almost cracked. "After they were bought, I mean."

"Three of them." Darius wouldn't look up from the notes he was making. Without appearing physically tense, it was still there in the air. He was on edge. "No, I won't tell you their names."

"Why?"

"Because you don't want to know." He reminded Gray to eat again with another pointed look. "Which of the kids would you say aren't as equipped to deal with the torture as the rest of you?"

Worst topic to have over breakfast. Nausea crept up Gray's throat, and the smell of bacon nearly did him in. Swallowing past the bile, he jammed two pieces into his mouth and chewed slowly.

"Milo, Jackie—"

"Jackie's owner is lonely and craves affection. He's not a sadist. He's a pedophile who deserves a bullet in the head, but right now, Jackie's not the one suffering the most. Not mentally or physically."

Okay, but...he'd asked who could withstand the least number of beatings, and Gray had answered. He watched Darius jot down Milo's name, which meant the disgusting son of a bitch who'd stolen his freedom was worse.

"Charlie," Gray said quietly. "They put a tracker in him—a chip or something."

Darius nodded slowly, writing it down. "What can you tell me about Oscar and Lee? They have the same buyer."

Gray didn't know much about them. They'd been quiet for the most part. "They weren't in the truck very long. I think they got on the week before Cole. Lee has nightmares—like, he talks in his sleep. Or cries—"

"Which one is it?" Darius looked him in the eye. "Cry or talk."

Gray frowned. Did it fucking matter? "Um, he cries out. It wakes him up. I think he's been away from home the longest—or he's from the South, maybe." Though, he didn't have an accent. "I heard him talk to Cole once about being chained to a post outside in three-digit heat, so I'm thinking he was taken before summer."

It wouldn't surprise him anyway. Lee used to play football, and now he was almost as scrawny as Milo. The latter was the one who didn't fit into the whole athletic-build criteria, but Gray guessed the kid's age trumped everything. What'd he gone for, two million dollars? It was insane.

"All right." Darius scribbled something else, then reached for his cigarettes and opened the window. "Who would you say are the strongest?" He'd lowered his voice, and Gray flicked a glance at the window. The ocean was below. No one could hear them, right?

"Probably Cole and me." Gray carefully touched a sore spot under his eye. He didn't want to look in the mirror today. "If I can get close to him, we can get his help. I trust him. He's more level-headed than me too."

Darius was shaking his head while studying his notes. "This stays between you and me for as long as possible. I spent weeks learning about you. I don't know enough about the other kids to rely on them."

That sparked some curiosity. "What, you were just sitting at home studying me until that little pager went off?"

"No, I've spent the past two months on the road." Darius inhaled from his cigarette and circled a name or a word on the notepad. Which one, Gray couldn't see. "I had to find the location of the auction, and the real buyer wasn't talkative enough. The pager only tells me when."

"So how did you find me?"

"That's a story for another day."

For fuck's sake. Gray scowled and chewed on a piece of pineapple. "Can you at least tell me if you had help? Or are we alone in this clusterfuck?"

Darius watched him briefly, maybe deciding whether or not to answer. "We're alone at the moment, but yes, I have help." *Have.* Present tense. "The buyers get searched before boarding, so the trick was to already have what I needed on the boat when I got on. My brother helped with that."

It raised countless questions, but for now, Gray asked only one. "Does my mom know you've found me?"

Darius's expression sobered. His eyes lost some of their sharpness. "She knows."

Gray nodded and looked down as the pain seared its way through his chest. He *had* to get back to her. It was so difficult to picture his old life now, but not her. Mom was always vivid in his mind.

"Can I ask—"

"Gray." Darius sat forward and gave Gray's shoulder a squeeze. Looking up, Gray saw the understanding in Darius's eyes. "Once we get out of here, I'll answer any question you might have. Okay? Right now, you gotta focus. We have work to do."

We have work to do.

Gray released a breath and slumped back in his seat. For one moment, he was left raw and open. All it took was a memory of home, or of his mother and brothers. How far along was his stepsister now? Jack must be over the moon to become a dad. Was Aiden writing a new book? Gray's stepdad was a bit of a hero, and Gray'd had to put a lid on his inner fanboy when learning his mom's boyfriend was one of his favorite authors. If only they knew how passionate Gray had once been about Aiden Roe's works.

None of that mattered now, Gray reminded himself. Yesterday, Darius had told him there would be no going back to normal.

Hopefully, he was wrong.

06

"I'm gonna have to fuck you today."

Gray reeled from Darius's comment at breakfast. Gray was gonna be pushed past his limits for this. It was sinking in now as they entered the dungeon on the second floor. It had to be right below their stateroom, or close to it.

He walked a little behind Darius, who'd only put on a wifebeater to go with his dress pants. Bare feet, belt unbuckled. Gray couldn't remember what actual clothes felt like. He'd worn nothing other than underwear since his fucked-up physical.

They'd spent the morning talking about everything that had to do with their situation, from what they knew of the boys and the buyers, to the mapping out of the yacht. Darius had a mad amount of info already, causing Gray to backtrack in his head. They hadn't discussed *everything* about their situation. Someone in particular was keeping secrets.

"I'm gonna have to fuck you today."

It was early in the day; lunch hadn't been served yet, and only two other people were in the dungeon. The sleek, lavish interior of the rest of the yacht was a distant memory down here, replaced by walls padded in black leather, a couple coffee tables that were also steel cages, contraptions Gray had only seen when his best friend took him to that kink club in Seattle... Except, this fucking-machine had a rifle attached at the grip instead of a dildo, the St. Andrew's cross on the wall was circled in barbed wire, and—fuck. Gray swallowed hard at the sight of a black-painted mechanical bull. *Cruelest sense of humor.* When someone fell off of it, they'd land on a spike mat.

"I'm gonna have to fuck you today."

Gray shuffled closer to Darius and passed some other equipment. It was best he didn't know what torture they inflicted.

One of the sick bastards was face-fucking Linus, an eighteen-year-old guy from the Midwest with freckles.

Darius draped an arm around Gray's shoulders. "Mind if we watch?"

The tall, slender sadist spared them a glance and gestured at the seating area in another corner. "By all means, I'm just giving my toy a reward."

It didn't look like a reward. Linus was choking and had tears streaming down his face, and Gray averted his gaze. That *couldn't* be sex. How many times had Gray gotten down on his knees to have his throat fucked? How many times had he almost come from it?Shame and disgust slithered into his body.

Darius kept Gray close once they were seated on a couch, and he pressed a kiss to Gray's temple. "Do you see the tall cabinet behind the kid?" He lingered, under the guise of nuzzling Gray's jaw. "There's a crowbar and a plastic bag with a thin wire stashed on top of it."

Gray didn't respond, trying to shut out the sounds of Linus gagging. The suffering reverberated in his head, and it was as if the crack in his chest kept getting wider and wider. *I used to love that sound. I'm fucking sick.* The son of a bitch grunted out his orgasm before pushing Linus away so he landed in a heap on the floor.

"Kill me," Linus rasped. "Please kill me."

Gray's eyes welled up, and he balled his hands into fists.

The buyer chuckled at Linus and zipped up his pants.

"Hey." Darius gripped Gray's jaw tightly and gave him a hard stare. "You wanna get out of here?" he whispered. "Then you better fucking control yourself."

Gray wrenched away and glared at him. Darius didn't know what it was like. For months, Gray and the others had been treated like cattle. This was the slaughterhouse, and rather than being turned into steaks and burgers, they were violated, abused, and degraded.

Darius had told him he needed a day to watch the others and collect the items his brother had left on the boat for him. He'd told Gray they'd have to make their presence look legit.

"I'm gonna have to fuck you today."

"What do you want me to do?" Gray tried to collect himself and focus, but the anger and the repulsion simmered just below the surface. He wanted nothing more than to torch this whole boat.

"I want you to remember." Darius exchanged the roughness for something almost tender and stroked Gray's cheek. Gray frowned and found himself trapped in the temperate severity of Darius's gaze. "I'm gonna show you where my brother's hidden shit so we can defend ourselves. Now, don't look. What did I say was on top of that cabinet?"

Gray swallowed uneasily. "Um, a crowbar. And a wire."

Darius inclined his head and leaned forward, pressing a lingering kiss to Gray's jaw. "Everything we do is under scrutiny. Our cover's secured, but we have their interest, and they have cameras everywhere."

Fuck. Gray hadn't even thought of that. Nerves tightened his gut. "How should I act?"

"The way you are now is fine. They see a man with an eye for mental sadism earning back your trust. It'll leave room for your emotional tantrums."

Gray's glare was back in an instant, and he backed away from Darius, who looked mildly amused.

"Case in point." He stood up and offered a hand to Gray. "You're the skittish animal who wants to believe me, but every now and then, you back off in anger." He paused to give Linus's owner a nod as they passed on their way out. All Gray heard was the tremor in Linus's choked cries. "Let's go, knucklehead."

Gray ignored the proffered hand but rose to his feet.

They were going to the top deck next, and Gray soon learned it was where most of the "guests" were gathered. A handful of men sat at the table where dinner had been served yesterday. It looked like they were playing cards.

There was a bar set up. Two young men were serving drinks.

The pool across the deck completed the postcard-worthy scene that made this whole thing look like a luxurious vacation.

Except for the part where two or three—make that four—boys were kept here against their will. Gray spotted Cole and Jackie chained to the slave posts. Charlie was kneeling behind his buyer's chair, and he was naked. Lastly, Lee was in the pool with the man who'd bought him and Oscar.

Milo wasn't here.

Neither were Red and her psycho son.

Darius picked a chair near the pool and shifted it to face the sun. He was just another man enjoying his vacation. Then he stripped off his pants and beater, leaving him in the same brand of black boxer briefs as Gray.

A young guy hurried over, his pale skin having turned pink around his shoulders and neck. He wouldn't make eye contact. "Can I get you a drink, sir?"

Darius studied him while he folded his pants over the backrest of the lounger. "Are you allowed to play with the guests, boy?"

Gray shot him a look. What the fuck was he planning? Leave the boy be. It didn't take a genius to see the waitstaff was here against their will too.

"The staff is at your service for your desires, sir," the guy replied softly.

"Hm." Darius got comfortable on the bed and parted his legs, one knee pulled up. "Six shots of vodka and a bottle of sunscreen for now." He patted the spot between his legs for Gray. "Have a seat."

The waiter scurried off, and Gray reluctantly sat down with Darius.

"What're you up to?" He furrowed his brow at the man.

"Getting a head count. Valerie referred to the waiters as the CD crew, and I didn't think she was talking about cross-dressers."

Gray snorted under his breath and leaned back against Darius's chest.

"Collateral damage," Darius murmured. "That's what it stands for. I wanted him to confirm they're instructed to let the owners use them. Now I know, and it might give us leverage."

"*How?*" Gray was horrified to think what collateral damage meant. Like, they were necessary, but if an owner accidentally killed one, it was worth it?

"There are approximately thirty-five people on board," Darius replied quietly. "Just knowing the waitstaff of at least eight isn't part of the enemy means less resistance." The last word got stuck in Gray's head, maybe because it wasn't until now that it hit him there would be resistance. Christ, he was dumb. What'd he expect? That they'd sneak out of here undetected? "Moreover, they're probably not as fragile as the rest of you. Chances are they've been around a minute."

Gray grimaced. *Fragile. Fuck you.*

"I saw that." Darius dipped down and nipped at Gray's

neck. The act was rattling. As if this was something to be playful about. "Put your pride aside, okay?"

Fuck you, fuck you, fuck you. "Sure." He looked away and folded his arms over his chest as the waiter returned with a tray.

Darius threw back a shot of vodka and directed the waiter to rub lotion on him.

All Gray wanted to do was apologize.

"What's your name, boy?" Darius asked.

Uncertainty flicked past in the guy's eyes, and he poured some lotion into his hand. "Excuse my stupidity, do you mean my actual name?"

"That's the one."

"J-Jonas, sir. But it can be whatever you like."

Gray leaned forward and averted his gaze again. He couldn't stomach this. The guy, Jonas, began rubbing the lotion onto Darius's chest and shoulders. Gray wanted to fucking cry. How defeated were you if you were willing to change your name for someone else? How *fragile* were you?

"How did you get a job here, Jonas?" Darius asked.

"I-I applied," Jonas answered shakily.

Gray scrubbed at his face, the sun beating down on him. Even though he realized Darius was doing this for a reason, to dig up information, it was sickening.

"Look at me, boy." Darius's low command carried enough authority for both Gray and Jonas to stiffen. Jonas probably obeyed too. Gray couldn't exactly see what was going on behind his back. "Do you want to go home?"

Holy fuck, *what* was Darius *doing*?

"I d-don't understand," Jonas stammered. "I can't go home."

"Why?" Darius wondered.

There was a stretch of tense silence, after which something changed. There was a shift in the air, and Jonas seemed to relax. Or more accurately, power down.

The next time he spoke, his voice was dead. Quiet, devoid of emotion. "I'm lucky to have this job. They take care of me here. They saved me."

"That was a nice script, Jonas. You can go back to the bar."

"Yes, sir." Jonas stood up, keeping his gaze downcast, and left.

Instructed to get on his feet, Gray left the lounger and watched Darius turn his back on the deck. There was a silent order for Gray to take his vacated seat, and he sat down awkwardly, ass on the lounger, legs snaked halfway around Darius's hips.

Darius scooted closer and handed over the bottle of sunscreen. "Are you focused?"

Gray nodded, though he'd needed the reminder. Even more so now when he was up close with Darius's chest for the first time. He hadn't been able to see the design of his tattoo before; now he did. Darius's right pec and shoulder were filled with hundreds of digits and what looked like signatures. Some were dates, judging by the format. Some were bigger than others. The styles varied, though most of them were plain typewriter fonts.

A spark of attraction ignited as Gray took over from Jonas and rubbed in the lotion. He'd have to be dead before he stopped acknowledging looks, and Darius had them in spades. It wasn't the first time he thought…in another time and place, Jesus Christ. Gray would've flirted his ass off.

"The supply closet behind the bar," Darius said under his breath. "You see it?"

Gray flicked a glance that way, seeing two white doors built into a set of stairs. It led to a big platform with a huge sunbed on top. There was no one up there now.

"Yes." He brushed his hands up Darius's shoulders and neck.

"There's an inflatable lifeboat in there." Darius continued

speaking, his voice quiet. "It will be our second exit strategy if the first one fails." He paused. "Ryan hid some gear behind the raft—a gun, survival shit, first aid." Ryan was Darius's brother, Gray assumed. "If I send you up here because we're leaving, all you do is throw the thing into the ocean before you jump in yourself. The kit Ryan put together is attached to the boat."

"Got it." Gray nodded again and accidentally glimpsed a couple of the other men. "Um, the fuckers at the table are watching us."

"Of course they are. They can't figure me out." Darius took another shot of vodka and hissed at the burn. "I should probably placate them with some violence. Curiosity is one thing. Doubt is another."

This, Gray was prepared for. He could take a punch. It was one thing he was good at, he guessed. "Should I do something wrong so you have to punish me?"

"No, I'm saving that. Lean back a bit."

Gray braced himself and did as told, and the second his back touched the cushion, his head flew sideways from Darius backhanding him. Gray blinked, stunned. The pain didn't strike immediately, covered up by the thick shock.

"Did I say you could stop?" The anger in Darius's tone pierced through the ringing in Gray's ears, and it brought him back. His cheek was on fire, he tasted copper, and tears sprang to his eyes.

He sucked in a trembling breath and blinked rapidly. The tears didn't make sense. As much as it hurt, it was nothing to cry about. It was a physical reaction. Wiping his mouth on his arm, he saw a smear of blood, and he sat up straighter. He'd dropped the lotion, so he picked it up again.

The tremors in his hands were fake. An act. The fear wasn't, and it fucking killed Gray. He'd *known* the strike was coming, and Darius was here to rescue him. Why was he afraid? Why couldn't he look Darius in the eye now? Why did he feel so worthless?

"I'm sorry." He didn't know why he said that.

A couple chuckles rang out from over by the table, and Gray eyed them discreetly to see he and Darius were losing the men's attention. They went back to their poker game or whatever it was.

Appeased by a bitch slap.

"I'm the one who's sorry." Darius cleared his throat. "Do you need a reminder of why I'm here?"

Yes, please. "No," Gray whispered.

Darius leaned closer and cupped Gray's jaw. "Listen to me, knucklehead. I'm gonna get you out of here, all right? In a few days, you'll see your family. If it's the last thing I do."

Gray closed his eyes and swallowed hard. A few days… He couldn't see it. Along with everything else in Gray's old life, the future was distant. He couldn't reach for it even in his mind. Or his wildest dreams.

Darius brushed his thumb over the split in Gray's bottom lip. Their foreheads touched, and soon after, Gray felt another touch. It was tentative and barely there, but Darius was kissing him.

"They're gonna think you're crazy," Gray breathed out. His heart rate picked up quickly, and he didn't know what to do. Did he kiss him back? Did he want to? Oh God, there was a part of him that did, and it was messed up. In under two days, his head had been fucked and manipulated one time too many.

"Unhinged," Darius murmured in agreement. "The crazier, the better." He wrapped Gray's fingers around the bottle of lotion and deepened the kiss. "This is the easy part, Gray. We get to fuck with their heads too."

If only Gray's head could be left out of it. As Darius swept his tongue into Gray's mouth, everything went hazy. A bizarre combination of confusion, fright, and need mingled in Gray's mind. Need for comfort, for affection, need to be treated like an equal, just…need. He found himself kissing Darius back cautiously, almost as if it were his first kiss ever. He was nervous and clueless and didn't know what to do about the heady emotions that built up.

Forcing his hands to comply, he poured more sunscreen into his palms. Darius grunted softly as the cold lotion touched his back, then relaxed and kissed Gray with more intensity. Practiced intensity. It wasn't real to Darius. Even when the kiss grew hotter, Gray could sense the absolute control Darius had of everything.

Gray explored Darius's back, the lotion quickly becoming an afterthought. Unlike Darius, Gray had no control whatsoever. He traced the scars and the muscles and kneaded the flesh, and panic made a quick appearance at the rapidly building lust.

"This is wrong," he said weakly, out of breath. "I can't enjoy this."

"Yes, you can." Darius threaded his fingers into Gray's hair and gave him another firm kiss, then slowed it down. "You know how magicians work, right? They distract us with a show over there so we don't notice what they're doing right here in front of us. This is our distraction, and it's okay to enjoy fucking them over."

Gray's hands fell to his lap, and he caught his breath with his forehead resting on Darius's shoulder.

A big distraction. Gray understood. They were gonna run hot and cold to the extremes, Darius being abusive and sadistic one second, only to be affectionate the next, and Gray was gonna eat it up.

All that aside, it wasn't the kind of enjoyment Gray had referred to. The embarrassment burned hotly because, in a place like this, he'd gotten turned on for a short moment.

"Come on. Let's get in the pool." Darius extended a vodka shot to Gray and downed his third. "I wanna get a better sense of Lee and Oscar's buyer."

Gray grimaced at the taste of vodka and squinted toward the pool. "Ouch." He stood up and touched the corner of his mouth. Vodka and open cuts were not a good mix. Wobbling over to the edge of the pool, he did his best to get his shit togeth—*what the...?* He swung his head toward the stairs, from where he suddenly heard shouting. The others noticed something was off too, and Darius appeared next to Gray in a millisecond.

"Get the little bastard!" someone yelled.

Gray's heart went through the roof, and he stiffened automatically. A beat later, Linus tripped and hit the landing of the stairs, where he quickly scrambled to his feet. He was a bloody mess, panting and crying, and he'd been severely beaten.

"You'll never fucking get me, you sick monster!" Linus shouted hoarsely. In an instant, everyone was alert; a couple guards drew weapons, one of the buyers demanded that the slave be captured, and Gray lurched forward without thinking. He had to help Linus. Someway, somehow. Gray's instincts took over completely and screamed for him to protect, protect, protect.

Linus was making a run for it. He slipped on a puddle of his own blood but managed to stay upright and dart closer to the railing. Oh fuck, no. Gray's eyes widened. Oh fuck, no!

"Linus, don't!" Gray rushed toward him but didn't get more than a few feet before a heavy hand landed across his neck and squeezed painfully. "Don't do it—fuck, lemme go!"

"Stop him!" a buyer bellowed.

"You don't take another goddamn step," Darius hissed in Gray's ear. It was followed by an equally painful grip on his jaw.

Unlike his restrained body, a world of fury was set free inside of Gray right as Linus reached the railing. Adrenaline overrode the panic and pumped in Gray's veins. There were no roles to play, only good and evil.

"I will die free!" Linus wiped at his bloodied and tear-stained cheek and climbed the railing, then turned briefly to Gray. Who watched in horror. *Don't do it, don't do it.* Gray's pleading expression met Linus's anguished one, and then he jumped overboard.

Gray collapsed internally as the spot where Linus had jumped flooded with men.

Linus's buyer reached them at that point and demanded a gun. "I don't care about your damn policy—someone hand me a sodding weapon!"

The pain in Gray's jaw became too much, and he sent an elbow straight into Darius's gut, then spun around and shoved at him. "You can fucking save him!" he whispered angrily. "Buy him—or, or, or kill the motherfucking buyer! Do *something*!"

Darius gave him a swift glare, a dark and murderous one, before he backhanded Gray hard across the face. "Think about what you're doing," he growled. For the second time in less than twenty minutes, Gray's head flew sideways, and his vision blackened.

"Control your properties!" another buyer shouted. The

Texan. At the sound of more yelling, from the guys Gray had been kidnapped with, the rage festered and gained strength.

All Gray could do was riot. He clenched his fists and took a swing at Darius, blinded by the emotions that'd taken over. Gray was fucking done. He wasn't a slave; he was a human fucking being, and he wasn't gonna take any more shit.

If it ended his life, he was going to punch himself free.

As he fought against Darius, the upper deck filled with more people. The impressions swam in Gray's head. Vanya ran out. Red was there too, and chaos had ensued. Benny appeared with a crossbow, one guard was restraining Linus's buyer, and there was a bizarre argument about the slave organization's policy of not allowing the buyers to be armed on board the boat.

Gray heaved a breath and blinked, registering the firm chest he was held against. Sweat burned in his eyes, and he tried to escape the blistering heat. He pushed at Darius fruitlessly and didn't recognize his own voice. He'd lost his mind. He hadn't been fighting worth a damn. He'd just been thrashing in Darius's arms like a weak, pathetic fool.

"Let me go," Gray rasped.

The defeat was crushing. His lungs squeezed. He was dizzy. Everything hurt. He couldn't trust himself anymore. Even if only for a second, he'd felt the power surging. He'd been fighting back...or so he'd thought.

Gray was a fucking idiot. He was no match.

He blinked past the emotions and caught sight of Charlie. The boy was kneeling in front of his buyer, eyes screwed shut, body trembling, tears falling, and he had a knife to his throat.

"He's not resisting!" Cole yelled at Charlie's owner.

Cole had been trying to wrench free from his restraints, judging by the blood seeping down his wrists.

"Kill me," Gray whispered raggedly. "I don't wanna live anymore."

Not in a universe where this sort of thing happened. The world was a horrible place.

Darius tightened his grip on Gray's sagging form but said nothing.

Gray only watched. The mayhem was being replaced by a sinister plan for "fun." Red allowed Linus's buyer to use the crossbow, and whoever drove the yacht set a course after Linus. He hadn't gotten far by any means, and the buyer was already aiming the weapon. There was a smile on his face as he took instructions for how to use the crossbow.

"We can still bring him back, dear," Red soothed.

"Fuck it," the buyer muttered. "I'll get another one."

Red and Vanya saw dollar signs and eased away.

"I can shoot him for you if you want, sir," Benny offered and brought out his gun.

The buyer smirked a little and shook his head. "Where's the fun in that? Let's place some bets, gentlemen. A thousand dollars on the leg."

Gray let out a choked breath. His chest hurt. Was he too young to have a heart attack? The pain fucking radiated.

Linus wasn't going to die a free man. He was going to be objectified once more and turned into a desperate target for sick, twisted, vile monsters.

"I'll take that bet," the Texan drawled.

"I can't watch." Gray swallowed against the rising bile. It traveled thickly up his throat, causing his mouth to water in warning.

Darius wouldn't have it. He ushered Gray closer to the railing and fisted Gray's hair. "That's exactly what you're gonna do. Look at him. Look at him swimming for his life."

Gray put a fist over his mouth, hurt and grief slashing through him. What kind of rotten, sadistic asshole was Darius?

Linus was some fifty feet away in the clear blue water that

continuously washed away the blood seeping from his wounds. His arms looked heavy, and his feet were no longer visible along the surface. He was already exhausted.

Three slave owners were taking turns shooting at him with a goddamn crossbow, each shot upping the money bets.

"You see what they're capable of?" Darius spoke quietly, and when Gray tried to turn away, Darius gripped his neck harder. "If you don't get your act together, that could be you. Or any of the other boys."

Gray closed his eyes as one of the arrows hit Linus, who cried out in agony. Blood gushed from his hip, and he couldn't remove the arrow.

"Let me die," Linus sobbed breathlessly.

The laughter around them, the humid salt in the air, the grip on his neck, and the pain pushed Gray past his limit. The nausea won, and he bowed over the railing and lost what was in his stomach. His eyes bulged and watered, his throat filling with the taste of acid. There wasn't much to throw up, and what little there was landed in the ocean below.

Kill me, kill me, kill me.

He was giving up. He could feel it in every part of his body. The fatigue was swallowing him whole.

"Too much for your toy, Mr. B?" Red teased.

Fuck you.

Gray coughed and gagged.

Linus was hit with another arrow. His choked pleas reverberated in Gray's skull like the worst migraine.

"I think I need to teach him a lesson," Darius said grimly. "I'd like to request the keys to the padded cell."

"Of course, handsome." Red snapped her fingers at a guard. "I take it we can't convince you to teach him that lesson in the dungeon? We'd love to witness your expertise."

"Next time." There was a smirk in Darius's voice, even as his tone held no room for argument whatsoever.

Gray wiped his mouth and stared blearily at Linus in the water. The other arrow had hit him in the back, and he was struggling to keep his head above the surface. By now, the yacht had obviously caught up with him, and the buyers were grinning down at him.

"You know, if we strung him up…" one said, trailing off suggestively.

Gray gagged again but managed not to puke. Behind him, Darius cursed, and then he was stalking toward the men with his fists clenched. Gray found himself with a few seconds worth of numbness and could only watch stoically. Darius lifted the gun from Benny's holster with practiced ease and aimed at Linus.

A shot went off, shattering the paralysis, and Gray heard himself scream, "No!"

Oh God, oh God, oh God. Gray saw Linus lose his fight. Darius had shot him in the head, and he began sinking slowly. Oh God, oh God, oh God. What had Darius *done*? Fuck, *why*?

"What'd you do that for?" the man who'd bought Linus was furious, though he stopped short when he noticed he had jack-shit on Darius in height and muscle. Darius towered over the man with a lethal look.

It silenced the others for a quick beat.

"Do you goddamn amateurs wanna get caught?" Darius stared the man down, never breaking the gaze, and pointed the gun at the horizon.

There was a boat. A fishing boat, maybe. It was too far away for Gray to see clearly.

"You seem to think we're alone out here." Darius clenched his jaw and took apart the gun like he'd done it a million times before. He probably had. "I don't know about you imbeciles, but

I don't plan on getting caught because you couldn't keep your slave on a fucking leash."

The guards relaxed marginally when Benny was given back the gun. Or the parts, rather.

Gray peered over the railing again and watched the water.

Linus was really dead. Darius had killed him.

Gray's bottom lip trembled, so he bit down on it.

Darius shot him in the head.

Red didn't want a fight between the buyers, especially not when her favorite Mr. B was part of it, and she was quick to get in the middle and smooth things over. After dinner, there would be some "fantastic entertainment," she promised. And Linus's buyer was reassured; he'd be moved up the list and invited to a new auction instantly.

Gray looked down when he felt a hand on his arm. It was Darius. His fingers wrapped around Gray's wrist.

"Let's go. Now."

Gray was too fucked in the head to do anything but follow.

The padded cell Darius had requested the key for was on the same deck as their stateroom, and it was exactly what it sounded like. No windows, no furniture, no nothing. Well...one lone spotlight. The walls, floor, and ceiling covered in padding and black leather. Just like the dungeon.

"It's safe to talk here," Darius grunted. He scrubbed his hands over his face, tense and visibly exhausted. His skin had a faint shine to it from the sunscreen, and there were a few scratches along his left thigh and both arms. Probably from when Gray had stupidly thought he'd fought the man bravely.

There was nothing brave about Gray.

"Out with it, kid," Darius said impatiently. "I killed your

friend. You wanna yell at me, so lemme have it. No one will hear us here."

Gray frowned and averted his gaze to an empty corner.

A shiver ran down his spine. The Caribbean sun took no prisoners, and regular room temperature felt chilly now.

"You shot an innocent guy in the head," he heard himself mumble.

There was despair and anger buried somewhere, but he couldn't grasp at anything.

"I ended his suffering."

That was one way of putting it...maybe. Gray wasn't sure. He was too tired. Too beaten.

Too broken.

"I have a kid brother... Lias. He's kinda like you." Darius slid down along a wall across the room and pulled up his knees, resting his forearms on them. "As a kid, he would try to save everything. Birds, rabbits, you name it."

Gray flicked an uncertain glance at Darius.

"He didn't understand that being softhearted is sometimes ten times worse." Darius lifted his gaze to meet Gray's. "Even when Pop made it clear to him that the animal wouldn't survive, Lias insisted on wrapping the creature in cut-up blankets and taking care of it. Feed it, comfort it...prolong its suffering."

Gray sat down silently in the opposite corner and pinched his bottom lip. In another life, he'd studied psychological dilemmas and theories like the one Darius was talking about. And surrounded by fellow students and a professor jotting things on the board, it was easy to make logical decisions. There, it was easy to end the life of a metaphor.

Linus wasn't fictional or an example, though. He was a real guy. Had been...

Gray rubbed at the sharp twinge in his chest.

He could see the last seconds of life leaving Linus. His pale skin, his freckles, the hair slick and plastered to his face, angry bruises, the silent plea to be unshackled. He could hear the coughs, the wheezy breaths, the whimpers, and the calm waves sloshing against the yacht.

Despite that, Gray knew he'd be too weak to pull the trigger. Despite knowing Linus was facing a more horrendous death than the one Darius had given him.

It reminded Gray of another thing he'd studied in college. The famous trolley problem. A train heading straight toward five people tied to the tracks... If you pulled a lever, the train would be redirected to another track, where only one person was stuck. You could choose to do nothing, resulting in the death of five people. Or you could pull the lever, the trigger, and kill one person.

Gray wanted to believe he'd have the guts to save the five people, but he couldn't be sure for shit. What he did know was that Darius wouldn't hesitate to pull the lever.

"Maybe I'm not worth saving." Gray's eyes welled up as the quiet words left him, and he kept his eyes trained on his lap.

What a fucking loser he was. And he hadn't even known. Hell, he'd always thought of himself as pretty strong. He'd stood up to bullies and defended those who couldn't defend themselves all throughout his school years. But what was a bully compared to those they were facing on this boat?

"I'm not cut out for this," he finished in a sad attempt to cover his shame with a joke.

"No one is," Darius murmured. "Not at first."

Yeah, maybe. Maybe. Either way... "I'm not gonna yell at you," Gray said tiredly. "I'm fucking clueless. I'm weak—"

"You've been through roughly three months of torture and degradation. Look at me, Gray."

Gray set his jaw and glanced up when he really wanted to cower away and hide.

Darius was dead serious. "If you wanna get off this boat with as many of the others as possible, I need your help. I gotta be able to count on you to see the bigger picture." He paused and scrubbed a hand over his mouth and jaw. "Shit might go sideways, and that's when you have to stay focused the most."

Gray nodded with a dip of his chin and cringed at the memory of his *Star Trek*-loving, closeted, married, hockey coach not-boyfriend back home. "I get it. The needs of the many and all that."

The reference flew by Darius's head, so he obviously didn't like *Star Trek*.

"Never mind," Gray muttered. The memory wasn't welcome anyway. It was pointless these days, much like his old problems. Back then, he'd been so distraught, downright depressed, because Craig had refused to divorce his wife. He'd wanted Gray to be his side piece. To think…Gray had spent months crying over that insignificant bullshit.

He blew out a breath and refocused, and there was no room for pride or dignity. He spoke with plain honesty. "I'm not strong enough, Darius. My mind jumps to random shit. I get distracted, I freak out, and I can't trust myself." *But…* With another breath, he let out the rest. "I think I can obey. I think I can direct all my attention to you and follow you like a dog."

Darius's features tightened with a slight frown, and he studied Gray for the longest time.

Gray wasn't kidding. He was a goddamn dog and not good for any leadership.

"You shit. You're actually giving up." Darius shook his head.

The accusation was a blow to the gut, and Gray looked down and wrung his hands in his lap. "I'm not…"

"No, you are." Darius was getting heated. "I was gonna bring you here to give you a verbal lashing for flipping out when the kid jumped. Then it ended the way it did, and I figured you'd wanna throw a tantrum. Now I see I gotta beat sense into you anyway. When was the last time you thought about your mother? Huh?"

Gray's eyes flashed with anger at that. "I think about her all the fucking time."

"Oh yeah?" Darius jumped to his feet and moved closer. "Well, I'll tell you what happens if you give up. I'm gonna have to fly home to your family and tell them you died. Your little brothers will grow up without you. Your sister's kid will never know you. Your mother will escape work whenever she thinks of you and start crying. Survival guilt will probably hit your older brother, and he'll beat himself up for no reason at all. Because he'll miss you so fucking much."

"Shut up," Gray growled, tears spilling over.

Darius wasn't done, though. "Your friends will have a memorial for you. Think of Abel... That little shit will be a mess." He squatted down and hooked a finger under Gray's chin, forcing him to meet his gaze. "Do you wanna see your family and friends again?"

Gray glared but jerked a small nod and wiped at his cheeks.

"Then you can't give up," Darius told him. "Not for a second." He stood up once more and nodded at the door. "Come on. Since you're not gonna yell at me, I can think of better things to do."

08

Half an hour later, they were back in their stateroom. Gray had showered and brushed his teeth, and Darius had ordered food. Several plates took up the middle of the bed, and Gray noticed it was mostly food that was stomach-friendly. Salads, whole grain toast, fruit, chicken, rice, and yogurt... He peered over the bed and eyed the cups of yogurt. Yogurt with applesauce.

"Easily digested and good for you," Darius said.

Gray nodded absently.

Having gotten so used to wearing only a pair of boxer briefs, he didn't bother asking for anything else. He got into bed and sat back against the headboard while Darius was doing something at the desk. One of those ominous briefcases was open, and a handful of pills had been crushed on a small mirror. The broken capsules lay next to a crumpled piece of paper.

"Are you gonna drug me again?" Gray got annoyed quickly.

"I hope not." Darius concentrated on pouring the fine powder into a tiny canister. Unlike Gray, he'd gotten dressed. Dress pants and undershirt. "If you need to dress your wounds, there's a kit here and in the bathroom. I don't like how your neck looked earlier."

"Probably because it's still infected." Gray snatched a yogurt cup and a spoon.

"Hm." Darius abandoned his task and opened the top drawer in the desk. "Luckily for you, I have antibiotics."

A pill bottle landed on the mattress next to Gray, who picked it up and retrieved one pill. "Thank you. Aren't you going to eat?"

"In a minute." Next, Darius stuck a syringe into another canister and drew a yellowish liquid from it. "Just making some preparations for our departure tomorrow night."

Gray's head snapped up at that. "Tomorrow? It's been settled?"

Darius nodded once. "I spoke to Valerie while you were in the shower. We're scheduled to dock around noon the day after tomorrow, and we gotta be outta here before then. I don't know how many men they have around the islands."

Nerves fluttered within Gray at this new information. Maybe there was a chance, after all. But he refused to think about it too much. If today had proved anything, it was how fast Gray could be jostled between resolution and utter defeat.

"We'll talk more about that later." Finished with whatever he'd been doing, Darius slipped the syringe and the powder into his suit jacket that hung over his chair. Then he joined Gray on the bed, getting comfortable along the foot of the mattress. "We have a few hours to kill before dinner, and I want to fuck with your head a bit."

Gray rolled his eyes and dipped his spoon into the yogurt. "You don't think my head's been messed with enough?"

"Not for this, I don't. You clearly react on emotion, so I wanna bring back your combative attitude by reminding you of everything you have to fight for."

The first spoonful of yogurt slid down Gray's throat, tasting like charcoal and reluctance. "I'm tired of feeling," he whispered. "It hurts too much."

Sympathy made another brief return to Darius's hazel eyes.

"If it gets you home, it'll be worth it, knucklehead." He started making himself a sandwich. "I'll ask the questions. Even if I know something already, I wanna hear it from you."

"All right," Gray replied warily.

Darius didn't fire off a question right away. While he took a bite from his sandwich, he pulled out a phone, and—wait. *Wait.*

"You have a *phone?*" Gray stared at him incredulously.

Darius's mouth twisted slightly as he scrolled on the device. "Even if there was any reception, they have a signal blocker on board."

Oh. Figures.

It looked brand-new, and Darius didn't seem too familiar with it. It struck Gray as a bit amusing, to be honest. So old-school. Darius could probably build a bomb with some rubber bands and soap, but a phone was alien.

"Are you like that MacGyver guy?" Gray chewed on a cherry tomato and watched the man frown at the phone. "My mom used to watch that show."

Darius's frown deepened at that, and he glanced up. "Good Christ, you're young. How old is your mother?"

"Forty-one. Why?"

Darius raised his brows before they dipped down and his attention returned to the phone, where he appeared to be trying to use a music app.

"Do you need help?"

"No, I got it." Eventually, anyway. A familiar song began to play, and Darius set the phone on the mattress. "This is your workout playlist if I'm not mistaken."

One of them, anyway. Darius must've copied it from Gray's laptop or phone. Did his phone still exist? Perhaps they'd found it on the ground after he'd been taken...?

Gray would have this song on repeat sometimes when he went running. Both versions of Dotan's song "Home" were awesome, but he preferred the first one. The folksy, spiritual, pop-rock song had everything he liked for a run along one of the countless hiking trails back home. A slow build, shiver-inducing background vocals, and a crescendo that ended with an "I'm at the top of the world" feeling.

Nothing cleared his head like a couple hours up his favorite mountain.

The trick when he ran up to Coho Pass was to break through the tree line just as the chase of the drums caught up with him and shot a bolt of adrenaline through him. He could feel his thighs burning and tingling at the faint memories.

He'd once done the trail with Abel, his best friend, and they'd reached the top of the mountain in one hour and fifty-four minutes. For regular people, it was a half-day trip. Hike up with a guide, eat lunch in the picnic park or at the restaurant, then take the tramway down. Gray and his mother had sent hundreds of tourists that way since she'd opened the inn.

Gray swallowed hard and blinked. He couldn't smell the fresh pine, the soil, or the forest air here. His salad bowl was forgotten in his lap.

"Eat, buddy," Darius murmured. "And tell me about your brothers. What are Gideon and Gabriel like?"

Gray let out a breath at the mention of his younger twin brothers. His stomach churned, his chest felt tight. "They're..." He had to clear his throat. "They're wild, I guess." Sometimes, you had to be sneaky to get the upper hand. Because no one could keep up with them otherwise. They harvested energy from anything and had no patience whatsoever. "They're not exactly the brains in the family." He indulged in a wry little smirk and forced down a piece of chicken. "Gabriel will probably be drafted next summer."

"He plays hockey, yeah?"

Gray nodded. "He's a great goalie. Abel told some scouts

from the Stars about him, and now he's got people from all over coming to check him out." Gid, if he ever got drafted, needed to work on his temper. He was fast as hell and a good winger, but he got heated quicker than an enforcer. No NHL team would spend millions on a forward who'd end up spending most of his time in the penalty box.

"So you have a best friend in the NHL. One brother might be heading that way. What about you? You're a hockey player too."

"Not on their level," Gray chuckled quietly. "I can give them a good run for their money, but we part ways where they live on steamed vegetables and protein powder and I stuff my face with a cheeseburger."

Darius's mouth turned up. "Abel may have mentioned that you're not the best at taking care of yourself."

Oh, please. "I took care of myself just fine," Gray scoffed. "He's extreme, and he shows his care in quirky ways."

Darius cocked his head. "What do you mean?"

This sort of got Gray going, because Abel had been such a big part of his life. "He's different. He has a lot of anxiety, so his feelings often come out in bursts. And they can get violent." Gray picked at his salad and felt the fond memories flooding him. "If I didn't get enough sleep or if I looked tired to him, he could punch me in the shoulder and yell at me. Because it upset him so much. He has bipolar too, and emotions aren't very easy for him to deal with. But once you tap into his language, and once you know you're one of his people, you have a brother for life. You'll know that when he's shouting at you to eat better and demand that you tell him all your problems, it's because he takes everything personally. He can't stand it when people he loves suffer. He will legit have a meltdown."

Darius hummed and nodded slowly. "He's an intense kid.

It's good he's got you and Madigan. Not many would get that involved in someone else's mental health."

"It's because of him I started thinking about studying more psychology," Gray admitted. "But I don't know. I kinda flunked at the end. I couldn't even choose a major." He'd spent his college years taking random classes and earning credits he wasn't sure could lead to anything. "For the longest time, I wanted to work with kids. Then I changed it to coaching. Then psychology..." He scratched the side of his head and shrugged with one shoulder. 'Cause it didn't matter anymore. "Anyway. Can I ask you questions too?"

"Hm. Sure." Darius narrowed his eyes. "But I reserve the right to shut you down if we get too off topic."

Gray snorted softly and polished off the last of the salad. "How many brothers and sisters do you have?" He was getting the impression Darius didn't come from a small family.

"I have three brothers who're alive. We lost Jake in Afghanistan." Darius uncapped a bottle of water and took a swig. "Two stubborn little sisters who have us all wrapped." He smiled faintly before he hid it. "They're the babies in the family."

"Usually how it goes, isn't it? With sisters, I mean." Not that Gray would know, having grown up surrounded by brothers. "Sorry to hear about Jake."

Darius dipped his chin in acknowledgment. "Willow and Elise are adopted, so they're not much older than you."

Huh. That was interesting. It was a pretty big gap. "How many of them have military backgrounds? And yeah, you're included in that bunch."

Darius narrowed his eyes again, but in the end, he went along with it. "Including Jake, three of us. I won't count Willow. She's just a nosy hacker." He paused, deliberating. "She helped us find the company that owns these yachts."

Gray lifted his brows. "She sounds badass. Your own intelligence department."

That made Darius smile, and he didn't hide it this time. "She's pretty hardcore. The rest of us are grunts. Jake followed in Pop's footsteps and joined the Army. Ryan became a Marine."

"Is it true what they say, once a Marine, always a Marine?"

"Oh yeah." Darius reached for his cigarettes. "It takes a special person to put up with a Marine. Luckily for him, he's got two."

"Huh?" Gray tilted his head before he connected the dots. "Oh...like, he's poly?"

"Don't get me involved in those new terms." Darius stuck a smoke between his lips and lit it up. "He's in a triad with his wife and another man, that's all I know. I reckon it's a good thing, what with all the kids they're popping out these days." He blew out some smoke and nodded at Gray. "Now we've strayed too far. Back to you. Tell me about Craig."

Gray blanched. Craig was the last person he wanted to discuss, and it was beginning to bother him just how much access Darius had had to Gray's personal life. He must've read private messages in order to know about Craig, 'cause the only person who knew about him was Abel. And Abel knew how to keep his mouth shut.

"What about him?" Gray asked stiffly.

"Touchy," Darius noted. "He's your boyfriend, ain't he?"

Or perhaps he hadn't read that many messages at all. Gray chewed on his lip, phrasing himself. But what it boiled down to was that he wanted to know what Darius knew. "You didn't read my texts, did you?" Because there was no forgetting the last messages he and Craig had exchanged. Once again, Gray had told Craig to divorce his wife if he wanted anything.

He could still hear the crunch as the phone hit the asphalt.

The two men who'd taken Gray had made sure he couldn't be tracked.

"Of course I did," Darius replied. "So did your mother."

Gray winced. "I didn't want her to see that."

"Why, 'cause the fucker's married? You stood your ground." Darius lifted a shoulder. "We had to go through everything, knucklehead."

Gray released a breath, frustrated and mildly irritated. "Then you know he's not my boyfriend."

"There's still a story."

"Not a very original one," Gray muttered. "I fell for my hockey coach. Turned out he was closeted and wanted me too, but he was married and kept postponing the divorce. Then the wife was diagnosed with cancer, and I deleted his number and switched hockey teams. Wife recovers, coach seeks out the gullible queer again, and the queer can't bring himself to stop messaging the coach."

"So he's a rat bastard."

And Gray was weak. Moving on.

"All right," Darius said. "I guess he wasn't the best approach. Tell me about your ma instead. You seem to have a special relationship with her."

"I was her favorite," Gray quipped. The humor was nowhere to be found, but it was a dig that had gotten Gid and Gabriel riled up so many times that it slipped out automatically. "It drove the twins up the wall when they missed out on pancake breakfasts in the garden. Like it was our fault they headed out at first light…?"

Darius merely studied Gray, brows pinched.

"She makes the best pancakes," Gray went on. "The thin ones—with lots of butter. Served with strawberry preserves she makes herself and whipped cream. *Man.*" He could go for a stack right now.

Leaving the bed, Darius flicked his cigarette out the window and then sat down on the edge of the desk with his arms folded over his chest. "Gray, do you realize you talk about yourself in the past tense?"

Gray frowned.

"Think back on what you said about being your mother's favorite," Darius said quietly. "You did the same when you talked about Abel. You speak as if you're never going home."

Gray lowered his gaze and didn't know what to think. Or what to say. He hadn't thought about how he spoke. Did he believe all hope was lost? Had he given up? No, he couldn't have. But maybe he was being careful. Maybe he was protecting the small flame that still flickered. His mind crashed at the slightest thing, and he couldn't take any more defeat.

"Perhaps you gotta mess with my head some more," he suggested lamely.

Darius shook his head grimly. "Not if even the smallest part of you has accepted a fate we gotta work against. That's not a mind-set we should cement—unless you wanna turn into a self-fulfilling prophecy." He went quiet, and Gray had no response. Darius spent the next minute or two clearing the bed, and he didn't speak until his back hit the mattress. Hands under his head, gaze aimed at the ceiling. "I admit, you're not as easy to figure out as I'd expected. Reminding you of your family clearly doesn't work."

"I'm sorry."

Darius sighed. "You have no fucking reason to apologize." He tipped his head in Gray's direction. "You think it'll help if I explain what we have to do tonight?"

The spark of interest wasn't nearly as big as it should be, but it was a start. "Only one way to find out, right?"

Gray could admit he was curious about the hows of the plan. Though, that quickly turned to dread when he thought of executing said plan. Was it even possible? Darius had said there were approximately thirty-five people on board.

"Tonight is about laying the groundwork." Darius sat up and mirrored Gray's position so they sat across from each other. "We'll be including two others today too."

"Cole?" Gray guessed.

"And Jonas from the staff. You didn't see how he reacted when Linus jumped overboard, but it settled it for me. I'll explain."

When dinnertime came around, not much had changed in the hope department. Gray remained crushed at his own weakness and resigned about the whole outcome. But there was something more useful than hope that Darius had managed to smash straight into Gray's soul. Determination.

He wasn't gonna go down without a fight, and he'd inflict as much damage as he could on the motherfuckers who deserved it.

Dinner was once again served on the upper deck, and Gray had work to do this time. Darius was a man who thought of multiple scenarios and created plans for each one, so it wasn't until they reached the deck that Gray knew what his first task would be.

There was a spot available next to where Cole was restrained.

Darius slipped a small baggie into Gray's hand, then ordered him to kneel by the slave posts.

The whole area was bathed in the rays from the sunset. Judging by the sounds of laughter and champagne glasses clinking, no one would know a boy was murdered here earlier.

Gray kneeled between Cole and Milo, and Darius bent over to shackle his wrists to the gleaming post. While doing so, he grabbed the baggie again, only to slip it into the waistband of Gray's underwear.

Gray had only gotten a glimpse of Milo, and it'd been enough to sicken him. The young boy could barely see; his eyes were almost swollen shut. Blood was trickling from his neck and ears, and his torso shifted in shades of blue and purple.

Gray swallowed hard as the heavy shackles circled his wrists.

"Be good for me, boy." Darius gave Gray's cheek a smack before aiming for the bar by the pool.

"We have drinks here, dear Mr. B," Red hollered.

Darius's steps faltered, and he threw the ugly bitch a smirk over his shoulder. "You don't have staff toys there, do you?"

"Oh." Red put a hand on her chest and laughed. The sight of her made Gray's hatred flare. "Right you are. Enjoy our selection, handsome." While she returned her attention to the men around the table, Darius reached the bar where Jonas stood stoically and ready to serve.

There was another guy from the staff too, and he was sent away.

"Are you okay?" Cole asked under his breath.

Gray stopped staring after Darius and faced forward instead. "Yeah. You?"

"I guess."

There was no use in saying no. Despite being living, breathing bruises, they were alive.

"Milo," Gray whispered.

"He won't answer," Cole replied quietly. "I've tried. I don't know if he can hear."

It didn't seem like it. The sick son of a bitch who'd bought Milo had aimed too much violence at his face. Robbing him of his senses.

"I need you to listen to me." Gray addressed Cole again and

eyed the table to make sure the others were occupied. "If I get the chance tonight in the dungeon, I'm going to throw myself at you to create a diversion. It's important you don't do anything to earn a punishment."

"Wait, what—"

"Please just listen," Gray whispered urgently. "We're getting out of here. You don't have to believe a word of what I'm saying, but there's a plan." He saw Cole stiffening in his periphery. If it was in disbelief or hope, Gray didn't know. "All I need from you is for you to keep your mouth shut. And I need to know as many stateroom numbers as possible. Where our guys are located, I mean. I gotta know the room numbers."

Cole let out a short breath, still tense. "You're not serious. Everyone knows your shithead owner fooled you, Gray. The fat fuck who bought me tried to do the same with me yesterday."

Gray ignored the sting of humiliation and scanned the dining table. Only one man fit the description of "fat fuck," and it would be the British guy. The one who'd complained that his slave didn't scream when having his fingers broken.

"You don't have to believe me," Gray repeated under his breath. "You won't lose squat by helping me, though. Just give me as many room numbers as you know, and don't move when I come at you later in the dungeon. You can even fight me off if you want."

Cole didn't reply.

Fuck. Licking his lips nervously, impatiently, Gray let his gaze travel across the deck to the bar where Darius was speaking to Jonas. The guy was around Gray's age, he guessed. A bit shorter and more slender, though he still managed to look hardened. His sharp features and closely cropped hair helped. His movements were methodical and fluid, and he mixed drinks while listening to what Darius said. Every now and then, Jonas would nod hesitantly or shake his head minutely.

Three servers appeared with carts full of food, and it raised the hum of the conversations flowing at the table.

Gray winced and shifted on his knees. Being so battered and bruised meant he couldn't hold a position for long, and his knees were starting to protest by sending sharp bolts of pain up his thighs.

"Lee, Oscar, and I are always restrained," Cole whispered. Gray caught himself right before he could whip his head in Cole's direction. "Philip—the bastard who bought me... He wouldn't be a match for me, and he knows it. A guard escorts us wherever we go. Same with Lee and Oscar's owner, since he's dealing with two. I don't know his name, but their cabin is next to ours—number eight. I'm in nine."

Gray swallowed and stored the information. Darius had shown him a rough drawing of the map of the yacht, and if it was correct, staterooms eight and nine were on the other side of the boat, same floor as Darius and Gray's cabin.

One guard patrolled each deck at night. Evidently, Darius had been busy the two nights Gray had been drugged.

Something moved in the corner of his eye, and Gray adjusted his gaze enough to see it was Jonas who was walking toward him. This was it. They were about to find out if Darius was right, that'd he'd seen fury in Jonas—directed at the guards—when Linus had jumped overboard.

Fury was good. Fury could turn a person into a lethal warrior.

A guard became alert at Jonas's approach, but Darius said it was all right. "I want to see if the pets have any chemistry." He took a sip of his whiskey and stayed by the bar for now, even as dinner was being served and the others were digging in.

A few weren't here, Gray noted, which wasn't too weird. The meals weren't mandatory to participate in.

Jonas slowed down before he reached Gray. The hesitancy

was written all over Jonas, something Darius had banked on. This was an opportunity for Jonas to ask Gray if Darius could be trusted, and Gray hoped it was enough.

Carefully, Jonas got down on one knee in front of Gray. His eyes were light brown and shone with every emotion Gray had seen countless times in the other guys who'd been taken. Except, Jonas had apparently been tricked into taking a job here. Same shit, really.

Darius was walking over. "Don't be shy, slave." Okay, maybe he wasn't coming here, after all. He passed the slave posts instead on his way to the table.

Jonas jumped slightly, then eased closer to Gray and coughed into his fist. "I'm...I'm supposed to touch you."

Gray dipped his chin once. Under the guise of entertaining a buyer who wanted to have some extra fun tonight, they were going to put on a minor display of touching one another. Well... Gray couldn't do much with his hands shackled. Either way, it would give them a sliver of time to talk. And for Jonas to take the drugs tucked into Gray's boxer briefs.

Jonas closed the distance and placed his hands cautiously on Gray's hips. His fingers were cold to the touch, and being so close revealed things Gray hadn't seen earlier today. Like the scars on Jonas's torso. Like his ribs showing, the shadows under his eyes, and the needle marks along his arms.

"Is Mr. B for real?" Jonas whispered, snaking his arms around Gray's middle.

"Yes." Gray slowly rested his forehead against Jonas's shoulder. "He's been showing me where he keeps guns hidden on board." Only a small lie, as he hadn't actually seen them. But he needed to convince Jonas. And Cole, for that matter. Without help, it'd be a lot harder to escape. "He's done this before," he added in a hushed tone. "My family knows him too. He was sent here to rescue me and as many as he could."

"Okay." Jonas sucked in a breath as he ghosted his fingers over an angry welt on Gray's back. "I have nothing more to lose. My life here is worthless. Tell me where the stuff is, and I'll help as best I can."

Relief hit Gray squarely in the chest, quickly followed by a generous dose of adrenaline. He hadn't anticipated the last one, but now it slithered through his veins.

"Waistband, left hip," he whispered. "Do you know how to distribute it?"

Jonas nodded slowly and dipped his fingers underneath the waistband until he found the plastic baggie. "Mr. B gave me instructions. I'll get it done."

Against Gray's will, those words gave him a sliver of hope. It terrified him. If he lost it again, he knew he wouldn't survive. He was hanging on by a thread as it was, and he didn't even know the last stages of the plan yet. He only knew the importance of tonight and how this had to be done right.

Jonas soon returned to his spot behind the bar, and it was up to him now. Fucking obviously, Darius had a Plan B and goddamn Plan Z, but he'd been up-front with Gray. They were putting most of their eggs in this basket.

Jonas was going to spike enough drinks to put eight men out of commission. Eight men would wake up tomorrow morning feeling like shit. They'd suspect food poisoning and spend more time with their heads in the toilet than keeping watch. It wouldn't take down the beast, but it would fracture a limb or two.

If Jonas pulled it off, the cocktail of drugs would be distributed between six guards and two buyers. Gray had requested Milo's and Charlie's owners, as they seemed particularly nasty.

"Are you actually serious?" Cole breathed out. "Is he here to save you? To save us?"

Gray side-eyed him subtly, only to catch Darius's look. To answer the silent question, Gray bowed his head and directed his attention to the floor. *Yes, it's been done.* The wait was gonna be another type of torture.

"Help us so we can go home," Gray murmured pleadingly to Cole, never lifting his gaze. "I don't know if it's gonna work, but my family did send him. It's the best chance we'll get, Cole."

"Shit." Cole blew out a breath, suddenly antsy. The fear clung to the air around him. "How can you know?"

"Does it fucking matter at this point?" Gray hissed quietly. "I'm scared too, but I'm not gonna spend my life in captivity. I trust him. And if this doesn't work, I'll find a way to kill myself."

An agonizing, sober thought hit him. If this didn't work...it meant all had failed and Darius was dead too. Because whether or not they'd manage to escape had nothing to do with the fact that not a bone in Gray's body believed Darius was a slave trader.

Cole didn't hesitate as long this time. "I'm in. I'm not sure I can believe it'll work, but I got nothin' to lose."

It was the same for all of them. It was all or nothing, and that thought gave him more pleasure than anything. Gray lifted his head slowly and scanned the faces of the handful of guards who were scattered around the deck. His mind clouded with something akin to sinister elation, fleeting as the feeling was.

The actual escape didn't matter when it came to the damage he'd inflict, did it? Not really. Because when he thought of it, this was it. He'd get away or die trying, and he couldn't fucking wait to smash their faces in.

Men who had nothing to lose...was there anything as dangerous and unpredictable?

Rather than heading for the dungeon after dinner, Gray was ushered back to their stateroom. He could sense something was wrong; Darius was tense, his jaw was set, and his grip on Gray's arm was tighter than usual.

For once, Gray stayed level. His determination hadn't faded, and he concentrated on his morbid fantasies of how to make the guards suffer.

As soon as the door was locked behind them, Darius cut straight to it. "We have a problem."

Gray folded his arms over his chest and pushed past the anxiousness. "What is it?"

"Valerie allowed Linus's buyer to leave earlier." Darius loosened his tie in short, impatient tugs, and his jaw ticked. "They're all about pleasing their esteemed fuckhead guests, so she pulled some strings so he could be taken to another auction." He threw the tie at the desk before he pinched the bridge of his nose. Gray steeled himself. "He wasn't alone. Jackie and his buyer were taken to the same auction."

Gray's arms fell to his sides. The defeat threatened to pull him under again, and he had to sit down on the edge of the bed and take deep breaths. *It's not the end of the world. When we get free, we can find Jackie. We'll bring him home too.* God, no one would believe that, much less Gray. At the same time, he *couldn't* believe it was over. He couldn't believe Jackie was lost.

He'd barely seen Jackie during this monstrous trip. Darius had mentioned that Jackie's buyer wasn't sadistic, that he was "just" a sick, lonely pervert. While there were hundreds of ways to break someone, Gray prayed the lack of violence would help Jackie survive longer. Until they could do something. Because there *had* to be something.

"Any other shitty news?" he asked dully.

"Unfortunately." Darius slumped down next to Gray and scrubbed at his face. He'd never looked so tired, and it tugged at

Gray. It rattled him too. It wasn't okay. Darius was a strong motherfucker. Everyone was counting on him. "They left on the yacht's tender along with three guards. Before dinner, three new guards showed up in another boat. Which means there are three new faces to worry about."

Gray's forehead creased. So there'd been...like, a guard change. "Does that mean problems for us? It's the same number."

"They'll be more alert." Darius planted his elbows on his knees and his chin on his linked knuckles. "They can't anticipate our moves or needs yet, so they'll be extra attentive—not to mention trigger-happy. Moreover, I don't know shit about them. I don't know whether they're hotheaded or calculating."

Okay, that was...problematic. *Shit, shit, shit.* No, where was the menacing fuck who was itching to plan revenge? Gray needed him back. They had Jonas! Jonas was gonna help out a lot. Cole was standing by too. They weren't alone. This had to work.

Gray swallowed hard and ran a hand through his hair. "Then we gotta come up with something. I can't afford to crash again. I wanna be useful." He shifted a little and wrapped his hands around Darius's bicep. "Tell me what to do, Darius. Things went smoothly with Jonas, and Cole's in. That's good news, right?"

Darius didn't answer, but he seemed to appreciate that Gray didn't immediately give up like the loser he was. In the meantime, as Darius observed him pensively, Gray clung. Literally and figuratively. He grasped at his resolve, and he held on to Darius's arm and dropped his forehead to his shoulder.

"Tell me what to do, tell me what to do," Gray whispered urgently. "I'll fight with everything I am, I fucking swear. I just want them all to die."

Darius sighed and surprised Gray, maybe himself too, by

pressing a kiss to Gray's hair. They both went still, and Darius didn't back off. And it became...okay. It was comforting. It was new territory. For a second, Gray felt like he was more equal. He wasn't a slave, even a pretend one. He was trying his damnedest to be Darius's partner so they could get the hell off this boat.

"It may have to come to that, knucklehead," Darius murmured. "I wanted this quick and easy, but I think we're shit outta luck on that. Tomorrow's gonna get messy."

"I'm ready for it." Gray eased off the bed and kneeled on the floor. He looked up imploringly, pleadingly. "You can count on me, I promise. I don't care how messy it gets."

Darius's eyes flashed with compassion, and he cupped the back of Gray's neck. "You've never killed anyone, Gray. It does something to you, no matter how much you hate your target."

Gray didn't respond, 'cause he'd be a dick to argue. Darius knew what he was doing, and Gray didn't. Even so, he didn't think he'd hesitate. Not for a millisecond.

He would have to prove himself.

Darius excused himself to take a quick shower, and it left Gray worried as hell. It also changed the direction of his thoughts. All he knew about Darius was the man he'd been these past couple of days. Strong, unyielding, on top of his game. And now...Gray had to consider what Darius kept to himself.

Gray sighed and got off the floor as the water started running in the bathroom. He hadn't been fair to Darius. Coming on board this boat to wait stealthily and play a part before getting away with one person was a lot different from orchestrating a rescue operation that involved...Christ, how many? There was Cole, Milo, Lee, Oscar, Charlie, and eight staff members who were kept here against their will. And Gray himself.

They'd lost Linus. Jackie was...who the fuck knew where.

Guilt struck Gray hard. He rubbed at his chest to ease the pressure, but it only got worse when he continued thinking back on the time they'd spent on this boat. He'd made everything Darius's job. His task to figure things out, his job to save everyone, his responsibility to plan it all. Meanwhile, just an hour on board had the ability to change Gray's entire view of the world, so he'd become a juvenile headcase whose moods and resolve changed constantly.

He had all the reasons, but he couldn't let it be his excuse. He had to help Darius. He had to be there for him.

A loud, shattering thump came from the bathroom; it was the sound of something solid breaking, and Gray flew toward the door before he even thought of it. His heart jumped up in his throat as he heard Darius's low voice.

"Every *fucking* time..."

Okay, well, no time like the present to start sharing the burden. Gray got nervous, and he fidgeted outside the door before he summoned the courage to knock.

"I'm fine. I'll be out soon," Darius muttered in response.

It wasn't good enough for Gray. The man obviously wasn't *fine*. Giving the doorknob a tentative twist, he noticed the door was unlocked, which was both a relief and something that hitched his anxiety. *You pussy. You were never afraid before.* Gray's mouth flattened into a thin line, and he opened the door out of sheer stubbornness to prove himself wrong.

He stopped short in the doorway.

Holy fuck.

He hadn't been prepared on any level. Darius wasn't in the shower, and there were no fogged-up walls to hide anything. He stood completely naked by the sink, hands gripping the edge of the counter. Face downcast.

The large crack in the mirror and the sight of blood on the floor made Gray's stomach flip. Darius was the image of breathtaking strength on the brink of collapse. Nobody should be allowed to be that sexy, so fucking *stunning*, but it was terrifying too. Gray needed Darius to remain strong, and now he could only hope his support would make a difference.

"I'm just waiting for the water to heat up. You can wait outside."

Gray ignored the lie, manned up, and approached Darius. He eyed the mirror briefly, then gently pried Darius's fingers from the death grip his injured hand had on the counter.

The cuts weren't too deep. Three of them graced his knuckles, and Gray brought them under the faucet and turned on the water.

Darius hissed under his breath and flexed his fingers.

"Tell me what you're the most worried about," Gray requested quietly. He washed the cuts carefully. "I wanna help. Let me in on the whole plan."

Darius clenched his jaw and breathed deeply through his nose. He'd straightened a bit but kept his eyes trained on the floor. "I don't know how to get sixteen people off this boat."

Sixteen…

Christ. "Only" fifteen more than he'd originally planned. There was no word for how stupid Gray had been. Not to mention ungrateful.

"Jonas and the staff…"

"Ten," Darius confirmed. "It was his stipulation for helping out, and we can't blame him for that. I probably would've tried to help them anyway."

Gray's mind spun, going over what little he knew of the original plan. Or plans, rather. Shutting off the water, he grabbed a fresh towel and cradled Darius's hand in it. He was careful with the pressure and checked the wounds to see if the bleeding started up again.

No stitches needed, thankfully.

"You said 'every fucking time' earlier," Gray murmured.

Darius lifted his head as if it weighed a ton and offered a tired, self-deprecating smirk. "I tell myself not to give a fuck. Not to get tangled up in attachments and guilt and the urge to do the right thing."

Gray flicked him a glance, and he could see it. He could see Darius putting up one hell of a front in order to stay practical and calculating. Who could forget Darius's attitude the morning after Gray's auction? Darius had only been in it for the money and so on.

"You make it sound like a bad thing to do what's right."

"It's what gets people killed."

Yikes. Gray didn't push it. He patted Darius's knuckles dry and discarded the towel. "Okay, so sixteen people. I guess that means the lifeboat is useless."

Darius nodded with a dip of his chin. "So is the tender. It ain't big enough."

And somehow taking both wouldn't work either. Unless they split up and Darius found more people he could rely on to lead. And they had to be realistic. Gray, Jonas, and Cole could probably pull their own weight, but when push came to shove, they were dealing with one strong, able-bodied soldier and sixteen scared-shitless punks. Splitting up would create more fear and uncertainty, because guards and other bastards could appear out of nowhere.

The yacht wasn't small. They couldn't know exactly when and where the coast was clear. Too many hiding spots—hmm. Gray cocked his head. Why did they have to flee and make themselves the prey? He chewed on the inside of his cheek and looked at Darius.

"Why try to escape unnoticed when we can attack unnoticed?"

Darius straightened further and furrowed his brow.

Gray clarified as the thoughts became clearer. "Instead of running and not knowing who's chasing us, we could attack them one by one." The idea grew on him fast. "You have guns and shit stashed around the boat, and there are countless cabins we can lock people inside of."

He could see the wheels turning in Darius's head. His eyes narrowed, and his gaze flickered while he studied Gray. Or maybe he was just focusing on Gray's face while his mind raced to come up with a strategy. That seemed more plausible.

"How much heroin do you have?" Gray wondered. "Can it be used to slow the others down?"

"Hmm. It works fast, but not that fast. We might find use for it, though." Darius turned around and leaned back against the edge of the counter, seemingly unbothered by his complete lack of cover-up. With the ideas surging and knowing that all hope wasn't lost, Gray found it just a bit more difficult to concentrate. A bit.

Leaving Darius's side, Gray crossed the bathroom to first turn off the water in the shower and then to sit down on the toilet lid. Well...fuck. Perhaps distance was no help at all when it put him face-to-crotch with Darius.

The man's cock was a work of art, that was all. The thick, soft length rested over and down his sac. The area was trimmed but not meticulously. And those thighs... Those balls, that cock, and those thighs. He was uncircumcised like Gray, which he had to admit he preferred. Few things were as sexy as the skin stretching around the shaft as it grew harder and harder, and —*what the fuck am I doing?*

Gray rolled his eyes at himself and looked away.

"I have to get into their control room," Darius said pensively. "They run surveillance in all common areas except the hallways, and if we're gonna be able to sneak up on the security, we need to kill the camera feed."

Gray cleared his throat and nodded, refocusing. "You need me to create a diversion tonight so you can get some of the guns your brother hid. Do you think it's possible to create one that's big enough that it gives you time and an excuse to step out for a few minutes?"

Darius hummed and rubbed his jaw. "It should be, but it would be the act that sets it all off. At that point, there's no going back. You'll need to be close to a way to defend yourself, 'cause you'll most likely need it before I can get back to you."

Made sense. Once the video cameras were off, it wouldn't be long before someone noticed.

"Well, I'm jumping Cole and disobeying you," Gray said. "Even though you don't need a reason, it's a solid excuse to give me one hell of a punishment. Make it public, and you'll have yourself a big audience." Then all Darius had to do was say he'd forgotten something in their stateroom and that he'd be right back.

Darius wasn't too sold on that idea, though he didn't dismiss it. "I'll think of something. I'd like to avoid hurting you more. That includes us fucking. I think we can avoid it if we play our cards right."

Gray lifted a shoulder. He didn't think physical pain could touch him anymore. His whole body had been hurting for three months, and he'd become a pro at breathing through it.

As for the fucking... No, best not to give it a single thought.

Darius pushed away from the counter and nodded at the door. "We're on to something now, knucklehead. You're not as stupid as you look." He smiled crookedly, a hot sight, and Gray snorted. "I'mma take a quick shower now."

Gray took the hint and stood up. Before tomorrow came around, they had a hellish night in the dungeon to endure, and it was a sobering thought. The suffering was far from over.

10

How many times could a plan change in forty-eight hours? However many times it fucking took, according to Darius. An answer that'd been accompanied by a weirdly be-good-for-me-or-else look.

It'd taken him ten minutes to shower—and switch gears so much that it made Gray dizzy. Now, forty minutes later, they walked into a packed dungeon with a new strategy, and Gray didn't even have to pretend to be lost. Thankfully, he was more reenergized with determination than ever, but fuck if he wasn't confused as shit.

He was no longer going to create a diversion by throwing himself at Cole. In fact, Darius was going to expose what his brother had risked a lot to hide. He was also going to "take advantage of Valerie's infatuation," whatever that meant.

"This is partly why I haven't let you in on the planning before," Darius had told him before they'd left the stateroom. "There's a reason I gotta come up with several scenarios. You know what they say, a plan never survives the first contact with the enemy."

Uh, no. Gray didn't know what "they" said…

So, who knew, maybe it would change again. For now, Gray stuck to the top tasks on their to-do list, and what he had to do tonight didn't suck that bad. Despite that he was unsure of the reasoning behind it.

The men in the dungeon were gathered around something—a large metal cage. It was a gut punch to see two of the staff guys inside, and judging by what Gray had heard from these fuckers before, the two in the cage weren't fighting for shits and giggles.

"Come on, now!" Red rapped her thin cane against the metal grid. "If this is how you fight for your lives, they can't be worth much!"

Gray's stomach lurched.

"Keep walking," Darius whispered and ushered him toward the seating area.

Industrial music blended with the gruff chuckles from the buyers and some of the guards. Whiskey was flowing, and the air was thick with sex and cologne. Jackets had been thrown off, ties had been loosened. Shirts untucked. Torture equipment had been pushed to the walls to make room for a monster cage that rattled every time the two boys inside shoved at each other.

Nearing the black leather couches, Gray made eye contact with Cole. Who was naked and panting and kneeling on the floor. Feet restrained and parted with a spreader bar, hands cuffed in front of him. Shame filled his eyes. The British guy—Philip...? He was zipping his pants.

Gray's heart broke for Cole, and he tried to convey all the promise he could with a look. "It'll be okay," he mouthed.

Cole swallowed hard and looked down.

"Mr. B," Philip greeted.

"Evening." Darius dipped his chin and got comfortable on one of the couches.

Gray sank down on his knees by Darius's feet.

"Valerie tried to wait for you," Philip mentioned. He

snapped his fingers to get the attention of one of the servers too. "At least you only missed the first fight. This one just started."

There'd been one before this? Christ, these savages had no limits.

"She didn't need to do that." Darius folded the sleeves of his button-down and gave the server a nod too. "Cage fighting isn't really my style." Once Philip had ordered, it was Darius's turn. "Tullamore, neat—and is Jonas around?"

The server bowed his head. "I'll get him for you, sir."

Gray flinched at the sound of a blood-curdling scream, and he tried to shut out the fight taking place less than fifteen feet away. Tilting his head toward Cole, he did a small double take when he saw something. Cole was dragging his finger across a tiny surface on the floor; he was drawing numbers.

Four.

Gray squinted and inched back slightly, enough to shift the glare from the spotlights to another digit. The floor was like the screen on any cell phone. Natural grease from the skin created faint marks that gleamed in the light, and Gray memorized every number. Four, five, eight, nine. Four, five, eight, nine. It must be the stateroom numbers Cole had managed to figure out.

Darius and Gray's cabin wasn't close to anybody else's that he knew. At least, he hadn't seen anyone come out or enter through the doors at the end of the hallway where their stateroom was. What he did know was their cabin number. Twelve.

Four, five, eight, nine, twelve. That was six buyers and seven hostages. Jackie was...somewhere else, and Linus... Right. So... yeah. Four, five, eight, nine, twelve.

He nodded discreetly at Cole, who let out a breath and wiped his hand over the markings.

Red's deep voice broke the moment. "My dear Mr. B, I was saddened you missed the first show." She sauntered over with the server and Jonas.

Darius accepted his drink and patted his stomach. "I'm afraid I wasn't feeling too well earlier."

"Oh no." For being such a sadistic cunt, she sure had a lot of sympathy for some people. She instantly sat down next to Darius and looked at him with concern. "Do you think it was something you ate?"

Gray kept them in his periphery.

"I hope not, because I ate a lot." Darius winked and touched Red's cheek, and the sight was like nails on a chalkboard to Gray. "I have quite the appetite."

Jesus Christ, Red actually blushed. "You're dangerous, handsome. How many women's hearts have you broken just by saying you're into men?"

Fuck you, you fucking hag.

The edges of Gray's vision blurred with hatred.

Darius chuckled in his rich voice. "Life is too short to limit yourself to one gender."

Oh, for chrissakes.

If he didn't have all of Red's attention before, he sure as fuck had it now. If she got any closer to him, she'd be on his lap. Well, guess that answered what Darius meant by taking advantage of Red's infatuation. He was going to fucking flirt with the bitch.

Gray tuned out her ugly giggles and Darius's low murmurs and surveyed the area. Jonas was the first person he saw, and he wondered if Darius even cared that he was the one who'd asked for the guy.

Jonas tested the smallest, most unsure smile, but Gray didn't need more than that. He returned the discreet smile, and just like that, he was closer to this guy than to most people he'd exchanged smiles with at home. Even people he'd call acquaintances. Or, hell, past flings and hookups.

Remembering he had a job to do, Gray flicked a glance at the glass of whiskey in Darius's hand before making eye contact with Jonas again. A silent question. Gray lifted a brow, and thank fuck, Jonas offered a quick nod. He'd distributed the drug already.

Gray blew out a breath and couldn't contain the relief. A full-fledged smile broke out.

The only thing that could kill it did so fast. A listless, bloody body was being dragged out of the metal cage, and the winner didn't have much to celebrate other than being alive. He'd been forced to beat the life out of someone who'd shared his fate on this forsaken yacht.

Gray caught the pain in Jonas's expression.

There wouldn't be sixteen people to save, after all. What were they down to now, fourteen?

Red's laughter at whatever Darius said made Gray's blood boil. The fury that simmered underneath the surface made up for lost muscle mass, it felt like. If given the green light, Gray would've tried to kill them all.

Fuck, how he hated the world.

The chuckles died down, and Red sighed contentedly and put a hand on Darius's thigh. "Unfortunately, work calls. There's one more fight to enjoy, but I'm all yours later. I'll give you a tour you won't forget anytime soon."

Barf.

"Sounds like a plan," Darius replied. "Perhaps we can discuss the next auction then too."

That was Gray's cue to pay attention.

"Oh?" Red leaned closer, curious. "Are you unhappy with your purchase or merely looking to expand your stable?"

Stable? Gray gnashed his teeth together.

Darius slipped his fingers into Gray's hair and yanked his head back. "I admit, this one was easier to break than I'd hoped. I was promised a hellion whose mind I could pull in and out of enslavement."

It took everything of Gray's self-control to keep from rolling his eyes, and Darius knew it. His eyes glinted with a bit of humor, giving Gray a new struggle. He was warming up to Darius so quickly, and the man was fucking beautiful. More than that, he was solid and offered comfort without realizing it. The period of doubting Darius was completely wiped away.

In the meantime, Red was apologizing profusely, stating she'd been so sure Gray was going to be a difficult toy. She also promised she'd speak to the management about another auction.

"Where's the closest one?" Darius asked curiously and released Gray. "There's one taking place tonight, isn't there?"

Red checked her diamond-encrusted watch and chuckled apologetically. "I fear I can't disclose the location, as I'm sure you understand. Our two guests who were taken there earlier should have arrived now, and they filled the last spots." She paused, the dumb cunt. She couldn't disclose the location, but she'd just given Darius a good estimate on the distance. "Are you that disappointed with your slave, sir?"

"It's not just that," Darius answered. "I'm always looking for bigger challenges. A second toy might make it more fun. Unless I dispose of this one and find one who can satisfy me properly."

And it was Gray's turn to speak. "Master, I can be rebellious for you."

"Sure you can," Darius chuckled. At his evident humor, Red allowed herself to laugh too.

"No, I swear." Gray turned around and put on the show of his life. He pleaded. "I can be a menace if you want. I'll prove it!" He scrambled to his feet and looked around. *Don't throw up.* The two dead boys from the previous fights had been stashed in a pile of limbs next to the mechanical bull with the spike mat.

"What do you think you're going to do, boy?" Darius looked on in amusement. "I broke you down in a day and a half."

"No, you didn't," Gray insisted. When he glanced out over

the dungeon again, he spotted Benny. *Ohfuckyes*. It was going to be difficult not to enjoy this. Gray had fucking earned this. And besides, he was *supposed* to do something that would "provoke." This should cut it.

He left Darius's side and pushed past a few men who were toasting to a good time. Benny was standing in the background with another guard, and he didn't see Gray until they were right in front of each other. Gray didn't even blink or gather any courage. It wasn't needed. He grabbed Benny's head and yanked it down as he kicked up his knee.

Adrenaline and satisfaction exploded within, and a hysterical little laugh bubbled up. "I can't fucking wait to kill you." His promise was drowned out by Benny's pained growl and the other guard's shout. Not a second passed before Gray had two guns aimed at his head, but it didn't bother him in the slightest. He could count on Darius.

Another guard had swooped in from somewhere, and he pressed the barrel of his gun to Gray's temple. "What the fuck do you think you're doing, you disrespectful little fuckhole?"

A silence had fallen over the dungeon, including the music.

Benny grunted as he straightened up, a hand cupping his nose. Blood gushed from between his fingers.

Gray grinned. On the one hand, he was empty on the inside. No fear, no pain, no dread. On the other hand, could he really be empty if there was elation, as skin-deep and temporary as it was?

"You're dead," Benny rasped.

"You might wanna run that by my owner first." Remembering he had a destination, Gray slowly shifted one gun away from him and took a step toward the cabinet farther to the left. "Excuse me. Dumb fucks."

"*Gray…*"

Gray faltered at the sound of Charlie. Kneeling by his

owner across the room, the boy was begging Gray with his eyes —begging him not to get into any trouble. But Charlie didn't have to worry. It was gonna be okay.

Closing the distance, Gray reached the cabinet and faced away from it. Darius had gotten off the couch, and he was the only one in the room who looked perfectly at ease. Red and most of the others were on edge, and a rotten minority had already jumped to the anticipation and enjoyment of the punishment.

"I'm gonna kill all of you," Gray said. He scratched the side of his head, then nodded at Red. "You…I wanna stab you with that fucking cane you're always carrying around. Maybe make your deranged son shove it up your dusty old pussy. You all make me sick, and you deserve to burn in hell."

"All right, that's enough, boy," Darius said mildly. "Nice act, but you're not fooling me. The minute we're back in our room, you'll be begging me to spare you."

"And you're not going to spare him, are you?" Red was seething, which she couldn't show Darius. He was an "esteemed guest," one with a lot of money. They came first, and Red's job was to please the guests. Even if it meant one buyer's toy smashing a guard's nose. Again.

Darius had talked about this earlier in passing. How everything on board was a power play. If you showed weakness, someone would take advantage.

So he wasn't going to let himself be bossed around for a second. "That's up to me, Valerie. Isn't it?" He gave Red a pointed look before leaving her side and moving toward Gray. "That said, I don't think any of you will be disappointed in what I have in store for my property."

Just like that, a collective whoosh traveled through the dungeon. The assertiveness was being restored, and the monsters were looking forward to watching Gray suffer.

Red smiled smugly.

Gray scratched his eyebrow with his middle finger.

Darius was more focused on one of the guards, the one who hadn't lowered his weapon yet, and it took Gray a couple seconds to realize another fucking plan had changed. Rather than shoving Gray up against the cabinet, Darius was going for the guard.

Gray stepped closer to the mechanical bull and winced at the spikes digging into the soles of his feet. In the meantime, Darius grabbed the guard by the lapels of his jacket and yoked him up, the whole cabinet rattling at the impact.

The tension in the dungeon made a swift return, and the guard's narrow, dark eyes grew wide.

"You put a gun to my slave boy's head." Darius leaned in and nipped at the dude's cheek, and Gray swallowed uneasily. He had Darius on his side, and the man still intimidated with his dominance and utter confidence. The guard had to be close to pissing himself. Darius was white-knuckling the guy's jaw, he was squeezing it so hard. "Another wrong move from you, and I'll make you my fuckhole instead. We clear?"

The guy grunted and struggled to stand on his toes, and he tried to look over at Red first. He was looking for support, but he wouldn't get it from the woman whose priority was the buyers' comfort.

"Are we clear?" Darius growled, and he slammed the guard against the cabinet once more. It was hard enough that Gray heard something moving, metal shifting on wood, on top of the cabinet. The crowbar.

No one else seemed to be paying any attention whatsoever to some random noise, but Darius threw the guy out of his way and aced the look of suspicion. He reached up and felt around the top, and Gray inched toward him to be of assistance.

"Is something wrong, dear?" Red asked. She stepped over the guy on the floor as if he weren't even there.

"You can say that." Darius's searching revealed the black crowbar, and he raised a brow at Red. "What the hell is this?"

"I..." Red was genuinely baffled, to no one's surprise.

"This can be used to kill someone." Darius wasn't fucking around with his anger tonight. His next target was Red, and together, they had everyone's attention. And at Darius's words, there was a murmur of agreement from the buyers. "What if one of the slaves had gotten his hands on it? Huh? And right here in the dungeon, to boot."

As he advanced on Red, Gray sidestepped to get behind Darius. He stood ready when one of Darius's hands appeared behind his back, and Gray quickly and discreetly took the plastic baggie with the thin wire. It was larger than he'd expected. But it did contain a long wire supposedly strong enough to choke someone, so in retrospect, he should've known the bag would've at least filled his palm.

Red had regained her composure, and she turned to address all her guests. "I assure you, gentlemen, we do not take this lightly. In fact, I'm going to have my men search through all common areas tonight."

Gray slipped the baggie inside his boxer briefs while no one was looking, the plastic sticking to his thigh. Charlie's buyer was one of the ones who had a wife on board, and he was particularly bothered by Darius's discovery. He said he was going to retire for the evening and that he wouldn't take part in any festivities until they could guarantee the safety of his wife.

There was so much Gray wanted to tell Charlie. The boy wept silently on their way out of the dungeon, and Gray fucking hated it. But, if Jonas had slipped the drugs into the right meals and drinks, Charlie would hopefully find some peace in the morning. According to Darius, the buyer's wife was a voyeur, not an active participant, unlike that other one...and where was she?

Maybe it'd been Linus's buyer who'd also had a female companion. It didn't matter at this point. It was an us-against-them situation, and Gray wasn't going to spare anyone.

He stood quietly behind Darius, as if seeking cover, while the others expressed their dismay at this turn of events. Gray found them all fucking ridiculous. It was as if they'd all been waiting for something to be less than perfect only so they'd have a reason to be upset. It was a goddamn crowbar, not a Molotov cocktail.

Considering Red's promise to search the common areas for weapons, Darius and Gray had work to do. On the small aft deck on the second level, Darius took a relaxing dip in the Jacuzzi, leaving his suit jacket to be used as a new hiding spot. As per Darius's instructions, Gray leaned against a wall where there was a small hatch to open. The inside wasn't much bigger than a lunch box—or first aid kit, in this case. There was also a gun, and Gray stealthily took it before stashing it in Darius's jacket.

The gun was heavier than he'd thought it would be. He'd never held one before.

He'd gone hunting a few times with his big brother, but they'd used rifles then.

"Are you sure the camera didn't catch it?" he asked quietly.

"I'm sure. Light's too poor out here." Darius walked up from the hot tub so they could continue.

In another common area, it was once again Darius who did the distracting. While Gray snatched two knives from underneath a cushy chair in a small seating area, Darius made arrangements with one of the guards. It was about Jonas. He was to be sent to their stateroom in a couple hours.

Gray rose from his position on the floor once he had the knives. He was keeping Darius's suit jacket draped over his arm now, providing a good place to hide the weapons.

"You know the staff isn't allowed to spend the night in the guests' suites, yes?" the guard said.

"That's fine," Darius replied dismissively. "No one touches him until tomorrow at lunch, though. I might speak to Valerie about buying him."

"Understood, sir. I'll make sure they know."

The top deck was the last spot, and Gray was fucking tired. Simultaneously, he was feeling better. Having something to do, accomplishing things, had always worked for him, and now it finally felt like they were on their way. They had dropped off three guns, seven knives, one wire, and three bottles of lighter fluid in their room, and they had an hour before Jonas was to arrive.

The deck was dark, aside from a few torches around the table and the underwater spotlights in the pool.

They weren't alone, they quickly discovered. Philip, the British guy, was drinking wine and playing cards with Vanya and an off-duty guard. At least Gray guessed so, given the man's casual clothes. All the others who worked security wore suits.

"What do we do now?" Gray whispered.

The breeze and the lulling wash of the waves forced him to repeat himself, and Darius gestured toward the loungers.

"We block their path instead," he murmured. To explain what he meant, he pushed one chair to be in the way of the supply closet where Darius's brother had hidden the lifeboat and another gun. "With the number of bitch fits I've had tonight, they won't cross me."

Gray's mouth twitched.

A server arrived, reminding Gray how much they kept track of people here. He could see two cameras, conveniently located near the light sources. And didn't that just suck. It would make it more difficult to get the lifeboat out. Even when it wasn't inflated, it took up a lot more space than a damn gun.

"I think I'll have a look at the menu, actually." Darius sat down on the edge of the lounger and nodded at the menu tucked under the guy's arm. "Pet, you can take off my shirt."

"Yes, Sir Asshole." The words were out before Gray knew it, and at first, he couldn't believe it. The stuttered noise from the shocked server confirmed it, though, as did the dry look Darius sent him over his shoulder.

Gray pulled off a stiff, sheepish smile.

What did this mean? Was his humor returning? On a day where three young men had been brutally murdered, he was finding it appropriate to make jokes? Or had he finally lost his mind?

He furrowed his brow and worried his bottom lip as he put one knee on the lounger and began unbuttoning Darius's shirt. The last thing he should do was go through all the states of mind that'd claimed him since his auction, but morbid curiosity took him there anyway. In the span of...what, less than three days...? He'd been in hysterics, he'd felt the suffocating weight of defeat, he'd ridden on waves of delusional power trips, he'd been crippled by grief, and he'd hated with every fiber of his being.

The server left with Darius's order, and Gray eased back to await instructions.

Darius got comfortable with nothing but his dress pants on, and he held up an arm, a silent offering. Or order, Gray guessed.

It was weird. He lay down carefully and rested his head on

Darius's shoulder, and it was fucking *weird*. Darius slipped a hand down to hitch Gray's leg over Darius's thigh too, making it even weirder. They were getting comfortable, not like before. Not like when they sat on the other side of the pool earlier and they kissed. This was… Gray didn't know how to put it.

"You can relax, you know," Darius murmured.

Gray wasn't sure he could. Like they weren't playing, that was how it felt. He released a breath and tried to unclench. The security on the yacht would probably be more reluctant to interrupt if Gray and Darius made it look all intimate or whatever.

"We're just gonna lie here for an hour like this?" Gray tipped his head back to be able to make eye contact.

In the faint light from the pool, Darius's eyes looked greener, with golden flecks near the center. His laugh lines and crow's-feet were a little deeper. His day-old whiskers a bit sun-kissed.

"If only." He palmed Gray's cheek lightly, and his hazel gaze glinted with wry mirth. "I'm gonna have to freak you out in a few minutes by making it look like I'm fucking you."

Gray blinked. Oh…kay. Right, yeah, they were slave and owner, and owners liked to screw their property on occasion. Except, Darius had gone from saying they would absolutely fuck to…maybe they could avoid it, and now it was "make it look."

"All right." Gray wasn't the flirty, carefree guy he'd once been. The guy who'd jump Darius at the first opportunity. He *wasn't* that dude anymore, and considering everything going on around them, it was downright sick to want it. No matter how small that part of his mind was.

He could erase the last time.

Gray flinched internally and closed his eyes. What was that fucker's name, again…? Billy. No, Bob. *Bob*. Fucking gag. He'd made Gray feel absolutely worthless in a single night, and all he'd used were his hands and a glass bottle.

"If you don't beg for more, I'm gonna fucking kill you. Your mom will find you just like this."

Gray bit down on his lip to keep it from trembling.

11

"Your order, sir."

Darius shifted in the lounger. "Put it on the table. Thanks." He rustled something. "Here."

Gray reluctantly opened his eyes and was met by a soda and a packet of Junior Mints.

It was the strangest sight, in a way. Soda and chocolate were something you ate at home. It was too ordinary.

"Ask me something. Anything you want about me," Darius said. "You get five questions."

That didn't exactly make this any less weird, though Gray was catching on. Darius was doing this to make Gray comfortable. Possibly to make him forget where they were for a moment.

Gray cleared his throat and sat up a bit, supporting himself on his elbow so he could take a sip of his soda. The tall glass glistened from the condensation, and the orange-flavored bubbles fizzled and made his nose tickle. He hadn't had a soda in months.

"Why do you call me knucklehead?" He figured he could start off lightly.

Darius chuckled under his breath and took a swig of the beer he'd ordered. "I guess it just came to me when I read through your social media and listened to what your brothers said about you when I met them."

It was a little unnerving that he knew so much about Gray.

Don't make the other four questions about yourself then, moron.

Gray drank some more from his soda and licked his lips. "Do you have a nickname? Can I call you Dare or something?"

It was funny how quickly Darius's expression flattened. "You definitely can't call me Dare. Ryan and Ethan used to call me that when we were kids. I always hated it."

Gray was gonna end up calling him Dare. "Okay, I have a follow-up question since you didn't really answer." He pushed forward before there was any silly protesting. "Are you the eldest?"

The questioned sobered Darius, and he nodded slowly. "I am now. Jake was two years older." That was the brother who'd died in Afghanistan. "Then it's me. Ryan and I are Irish twins, meaning we're less than a year apart. Ethan. Then Pop let our mother rest for a decade or so before Lias came along."

"And then they adopted your sisters after that," Gray finished, taking another swallow of his Fanta. It was so fucking delicious. He'd never appreciated the divinity of soda the way he should have before. "How old are you? By the way, that's also a follow-up."

Darius snorted but let it slide. Probably for the last time. "I'm forty-three."

Hot. It was something Gray shared with his best friend. He and Abel had always been drawn to older men.

"Family status?" It was a broad question that would hopefully give lots of answers, Gray thought cleverly to himself. "That includes kids, partners, the whole shebang."

Darius smirked, then wrapped his lips around the tip of the

bottle. Gray watched his Adam's apple work with each swallow, and it wasn't distracting at all.

"Ahh..." Darius set the bottle on the table. There was some other stuff there too. A paper bag, a bowl of peanuts. "No kids, no wife. I have an on-again-off-again relationship with a woman who works at my brother's gym in the Valley. But I reckon that's over and done with since she's ready for the wholesome family life."

And for some reason, he couldn't give her that...? Gray chewed on the inside of his cheek, debating what to ask next. There were several items he wanted to bring up that probably weren't important in the grand scheme of things. Like, was Darius straighter than an arrow or slightly...bent? Was he on Viagra right now? Did it bother him to be so close to Gray?

No, he could ask for something more meaningful. "Tell me three things most people don't know about you?" He leaned over Darius to set the empty glass on the table. The box of Junior Mints went there too. For now.

Darius hummed and coaxed Gray into his arms again. "Let's see... My parents split their time between Camassia and San Francisco these days, and when they're not home, I sometimes head over to finish Pop's list of things to do. He's forgetful, and Ma's pretty fucking demanding." He chuckled quietly and tilted his head toward the sky. "It just keeps the peace."

"Oh, wow... Who knew you'd be a pacifist?" Gray teased.

Darius scoffed. "Fuck pacifists. Cowards, the lot of 'em. They can sit around and sing kumbaya while others get the job done. Personally, I'd like to see how a bunch of hippies would manage when there are no diplomatic solutions. I'd get popcorn too."

That was almost a rant. Gray filed it away for later, 'cause at some point he wanted to dig. Cradled by the peaceful moment, he relaxed further and focused fully on Darius. He soaked up the raw beauty of Darius's features, the intoxicating masculinity, and the little imperfections that each had their own story.

It couldn't be safe to feel so comforted merely by someone's presence.

"I keep killing plants."

Gray's forehead creased, and he waited for Darius to look away from the sky.

"Now that I've got my new house, I wanna grow my own food." Maybe it'd been intended to be a light topic, but the more Darius spoke, the more bothered he became. "It shouldn't be that fucking hard to grow some tomatoes, but I managed to kill my last baby plant before I headed out to find you."

Gray stifled his grin and placed a hand on Darius's chest. "Baby plant? Are you referring to them as your children?"

He huffed in reply. "Get real, kid. No. I'm saying it wasn't old. It'd just started sporting leaves."

"Oh." Gray did the math and couldn't help but snicker. "Who grows vegetables in the winter? You'll probably succeed better if you do it in the spring."

"Why would that matter?" Darius frowned down at him. "You sow them indoors."

"And at a certain age, they gotta be transplanted to the outdoors," Gray replied with an easy smile. "My mom does this every year—around March, I think."

"Huh. Did not know that."

Gray let out a soft laugh and stretched out. The day was catching up with him, and he yawned. A salty wind breezed through, causing a shiver to run down his spine. It was the first time the Caribbean weather felt chilly.

Darius noticed and turned toward him. "They should come up here soon, unless they're doing a more thorough search."

"What if they haven't come up before Jonas gets sent to the cabin?"

"I'll think of something." Darius closed the last little distance so their bodies were aligned. "It's gonna be a long night no matter what. I have to meet up with Valerie too."

Gray made a face as he got comfortable, using Darius's bicep as his pillow. "What's the point of this stupid tour she's gonna give you?"

"Depends who you ask. She'll probably try to get laid. I want access to their surveillance system."

Gray cleared his throat and drew a finger aimlessly over Darius's pec. "I see." He didn't wanna talk about it anymore. He hadn't asked his five questions yet anyway, and that was more important. Also, didn't Darius have another random fact to confess?

A quiet chuckle rumbled from Darius, and Gray withdrew his hand and scowled, knowing he'd been caught. Been caught with *what*, he wasn't sure. He wasn't fucking jealous. That was irrational and insane and impossible.

Maybe he was afraid. And just a bit territorial? Which wasn't weird, he hoped. Darius was his way home.

"Look at me, knucklehead." It was as if Darius knew Gray would do no such thing, 'cause he had to hook two fingers under Gray's chin and lift his head. There was understanding and something burning hot swimming in Darius's eyes. "I get it. I know what this kind of trauma does to your mind. It's normal for a victim to latch on to the closest safe place." He carefully cupped Gray's jaw and pressed his lips to the corner of Gray's mouth. "You okay with this?"

Gray had stopped breathing and couldn't respond verbally, so he only nodded. He was more than okay with this. As their lips touched, something ignited in Gray. For a moment, he wanted to be normal. He wanted to pretend this wasn't an act, and he wanted to pretend he wasn't here.

"No one's watching, though," Gray whispered. "I don't

think those at the table give a damn."

"Good," Darius whispered back. "Then this part's just for us."

It made no sense; *he* made no sense, but Gray let it go and deepened the kiss. He teased the seam of Darius's mouth with the tip of his tongue, and he breathed in the heady scent of the man's cologne.

It only got more intense when their tongues met, and the heat consumed Gray quickly. He wasn't here on this yacht. He wasn't someone's property. He was somewhere else, where he had a choice, where his will was free, and he was making out with the sexiest man he'd seen.

There was nothing practiced or mechanical about this kiss. Darius was going all in, and it didn't take long before Gray found himself underneath him. The back of the lounger was lowered without the kiss ever breaking. Gray sucked in a breath and exhaled around a groan. His hands roamed Darius's back, his solid thighs, and up his incredible arms.

Desire shot through him at the feel of Darius's cock against his own. It was less of a surprise that Gray was getting hard, but Darius… Unless he'd taken a magic blue pill in the past three or four hours… Or he was fantasizing heavily about women right now. Did that even work?

Gray didn't care. Not right now. The bad memories were getting fuzzier and easier to push aside.

Swirling his tongue around Darius's, Gray slipped a hand between their bodies and felt around Darius's cock. *Oh God.* A full body shudder rocked Gray. He'd always loved the feel of a thick cock growing harder and harder. He made quick work of Darius's pants and pushed them down his hips.

"Jesus fuck." Darius drew a sharp breath and gripped Gray's jaw. Their foreheads touched, and the sheer hunger in Darius's eyes—

"Mr. B—oh. Ah... Sorry, sir, but we have to search—"

"Goddammit!" Darius growled furiously. "Can a man get some privacy around here?" In a second, he went from looking like he wanted to devour Gray, to wanting to fucking murder the two guards who now stood a couple loungers away.

Gray hid and reveled in the protection of Darius's body, and maybe he'd gone too far. He was too ravaged by need, so he kept kissing every inch of skin he could reach. Darius's neck, where he smelled fucking amazing, his shoulder, where Gray sank his teeth into the muscle and sucked at the flesh.

One of the guards got flustered, judging by the tremor in his voice, and Gray easily tuned the fucker out. 'Cause at the same time, Darius gave Gray a quick, drugging kiss and told him to get on his stomach.

Fuck yes.

We're not here. We're somewhere else. Just you and me.

As soon as Darius sat back on his heels, Gray stretched like a cat and rolled over, all too happy to shimmy out of his underwear. *You want it, so it's okay. It's okay. You have a choice.* He gasped as Darius's warm body covered him, his scruff tickling his neck.

"They're leaving," Darius whispered.

Gray grunted something and blinked through the haze. The two guards were by the table now, paying them no mind.

"I want it..." Even to Gray's ears, his plea sounded desperate.

Darius chuckled huskily. "Cocktease," he accused under his breath. Reaching over to the table, he turned the little paper bag upside down, and a bottle of lube tumbled out.

"Oh yeah," Gray exhaled. He rubbed his butt against Darius's crotch. "You gonna give me that big, beautiful cock now?"

Darius coughed. "What the—the mouth on you, boy."

Oh, whatever. Gray felt more like himself than he had in months. Could he have these minutes before they returned—*stop it*. Not going there. They had this moment.

He waited somewhat patiently while Darius lubed up his dick, and Gray squirmed every time he came in contact with the wetness. His own cock strained, trapped against the thin cushion.

We're not here. We're somewhere else. Just you and me.

He shivered and gusted out a long breath when he finally felt Darius between his legs. His long, thick, hard cock glided along Gray's ass cheeks, slowly pressing between.

"Stop teasing, Darius." Gray groaned and wriggled against the cock he wanted buried balls deep inside of him. "Please."

"I'm not the one doing the teasing here." Darius grazed his teeth along Gray's neck. "One of us has gotta have some self-restraint, so—fuck—so quit it. You have a fuckable little ass, knucklehead. If you keep moving like that, I won't be able to keep it at pretending."

Pretending? No...fuck pretending! Gray made a frustrated sound and shoved back firmly enough to make Darius ease off. Then he turned onto his back again and pulled Darius down on him for a hard kiss.

"If you want my ass, it's yours. I'm—" *begging you*. He froze for a millisecond. Kissing Darius, tasting him on his tongue, helped him relax once more. Okay, so he couldn't beg. The notion was all but revolting, but he did want it. He wanted Darius so fucking much.

He could make Gray forget.

"Fuck me," he whispered against Darius's lips. "The only thing I wanna pretend is that we're not here. We're somewhere else."

Understanding dawned in Darius's severe gaze. They were so close, noses almost touching, breaths mingling, bodies flush.

Gray could see the concerns Darius had. The extent of Gray's abuse these months, if there were any triggers, if this would cause more harm...but sometimes a quick fix was needed.

"Somewhere else." Darius's quiet echo of Gray's request settled it, and they'd run out of things to say. Their next kiss was slow and simmering with promise. It sent a heat wave through Gray, who melted underneath Darius.

Possibly not entirely convinced yet, Darius moved forward at a pace that should have been outlawed. He teased Gray's ass with his fingers, then the head of his cock, for half an eternity, until Gray couldn't help but puff out a breath and grin and ask if this was his first time.

Darius chuckled into a kiss. "Shut the fuck up, I'm tryna be a gentleman here."

"Well, it's not *my* first time..." Gray dug his heels into Darius's ass. "By the way, I'm shit out of luck if I'm supposed to look like I don't want this."

"We've done enough to secure our cover."

"That's gotta be the unsexiest way ever to tell someone you're wearing a condom...which you're not." Gray smiled to show he was kidding. And that it was literally the least of his worries.

"You really need to be quiet now." Darius knew exactly how to silence him too. He pushed forward in one long, slow thrust and buried himself.

Gray hauled in a breath and screwed his eyes shut. He clung to the fiery sensations, although he realized now Darius had been going slow for a goddamn reason. Holy fuck, he stretched him good.

"Christ," Darius hissed through clenched teeth.

"Mother of monster cocks," Gray gasped, shifting carefully to get another spark of delicious pain bolting through him. "Keep g-going."

Darius smirked against Gray's jaw, out of breath, and started moving unhurriedly. "You're something else, knucklehead. Are you okay?"

Gray nodded, slipping a hand between them to stroke himself. "As long as you don't stop."

There definitely wasn't any stopping. They found a rhythm, a seductive push and pull that finally swept Gray away from everything else. Darius had the most sensual moves, and he seemed to have a big appetite for Gray.

"Tell me where we are, Gray." Darius hooked his arm under Gray's leg and drove in deep.

Gray inhaled sharply and threw his head back, ripples of burning pleasure coursing through him. He blinked at the sky and thought he was seeing things at first. But the black canvas of the sky really was filled with stars. Millions and millions of glittering dots.

"Somewhere else," he whispered, pressing his lips to Darius's shoulder. "Holy fuck, that feels good. Again."

But Darius had something else in mind. They changed positions so Gray could be on top, and he sank down on Darius's cock with a breathy moan. Instantly, Darius's hands were all over Gray. In rough, greedy strokes, he manipulated Gray's flesh and kissed him just as hungrily.

There was laughter... *Red's here. She's at the table with the others...* Gray shook his head and silenced the background noise. Then he cupped Darius's jaw and threw himself into a passionate kiss. *We're not here. We're somewhere else. Just you and me.* He rolled his hips and took Darius's cock deep inside his ass, he sucked on Darius's bottom lip and traced the texture with the tip of his tongue, he felt the coarse rasp of Darius's scruff under his fingertips.

"You feel fucking incredible." Darius ran his hands down Gray's chest, up and down his thighs, and moved closer to his cock. "Use my hand." He circled his fingers around the base of Gray's dick and stroked upward until he could swipe his thumb over the wet tip.

Gray shuddered and wrapped his hands around Darius's, and he got completely lost. He took Darius deep on every shift of his body but kept it slow in an attempt to draw it out. He didn't want the moment to end. The kisses made everything foggy, and Darius's hands on him made him feel so fucking desired.

"I don't wanna be close already," he panted. He could feel it, all the sensations dropping lower and growing more powerful.

"I *shouldn't* be close already..." Darius was out of breath too, though it didn't stop him from ravaging Gray in another deep kiss. Breathing was overrated anyway, and Gray let himself be swept away by the euphoria.

He cupped Darius's cheeks, their tongues and breaths mingling, and rolled his hips hard to meet every thrust. Knowing that Darius was almost there pushed Gray closer to the brink.

"Come," Gray whispered. "I wanna feel you."

Darius groaned into the kiss, and his thighs tensed up. "Jesus Christ, Gray..." He circled his free arm around Gray and pulled him down on his cock, simultaneously stroking Gray off faster.

It was the urgency in the air that sent Gray flying. Darius's erratic breathing, his gritty curse, how his muscles flexed. The second Darius went under and started coming, Gray was surrendering too. The orgasm pummeled through him like the sweetest fucking relief.

We're not here. We're somewhere else. Just you and me.

Jonas was kneeling with his head bowed outside the door when Gray and Darius returned to their cabin.

A guard was standing there too, one whom Darius seemed pleased to see.

"Another night shift, I see." He smiled and shook hands with the guard, as if they were buddies.

"Yup, just started, sir." The guy chuckled and stifled a yawn. "I brought you your staff toy. Given the hour, Ms. Valerie could only allow two hours. I'll be back then to pick him up, and if you need medical assistance for him, just call ahead."

"I'll keep that in mind." Darius kept his face composed, which was more than anyone could say about Gray. He was sickened.

A reality check was what it was. The hour he'd spent on the top deck had given him a reprieve, and now they were back. He listened with one ear as the guard went on and advised Darius to keep his toys restrained, since there were two now, and that assistance was only a call away.

Jonas didn't look up even once.

"I thought I'd catch Valerie before she goes to bed," Darius said, opening the door to their suite. "Help me tie the pets."

Man, this really was gonna be a long night. Gray had hoped they could postpone the shit with Valerie till tomorrow.

Couldn't they have breakfast together instead? Why did they have to meet up at a time of the day when some tipsy bitches were looking to score?

"You wanna miss out on your playtime to see Valerie?" The guard quirked a grin but was quick to do as told. He got Jonas on his feet and aimed for the hooks next to the bathroom door in the stateroom. It was the same spot Gray had sat on the floor and eaten from a dog bowl.

"If I get my way, my fun with this little thing won't be temporary." Darius patted Jonas on the head before ushering Gray to the bed. "Valerie's the woman to see when you wanna discuss a price tag."

"Understood, sir." The guy secured Jonas to the wall while Gray ended up restrained to the bedpost on his side of the bed.

Darius slipped the key to the cuffs into Gray's hand. "Be good for me. I won't be long."

Gray nodded once and worried his bottom lip with his teeth. Despite reassurances, he wasn't sure they were in the clear from earlier. Occupying that lounger had possibly only delayed the search. Darius had seemed confident, but he couldn't be one hundred percent certain. He'd said he had studied the guards who worked that shift enough to know they'd just skip the little supply closet where the lifeboat was hidden. With the gun.

Darius had mentioned the shift change too, and that the new guys who worked during the night had other tasks to focus on.

Still. What if they found the stuff Darius's brother had hidden?

"Anything else you need from me, sir?" the guard asked.

Darius shook his head, only to think of something. "Actually, is everyone asleep? We were the last to leave the upper deck."

"A couple gentlemen are gathered on the aft deck for brandy and cigars."

"Thank you." Darius dismissed the guard and closed the door, though he didn't let go of the handle. He gave Gray a pointed look. "You know what to do, yeah?"

Gray nodded. "Unless the plans have changed again."

"No, smartass, they haven't changed." His mouth twisted up a little. "I'll be back as soon as I can—and quit worrying about the lifeboat."

"How come *you* aren't worried?" Gray blurted out, because he didn't get it.

To Darius's credit, he didn't lose his patience. Instead, he walked over and squatted down in front of Gray. "You have to consider the leap, knucklehead. Valerie ordered that search to appease us, not because she's actually worried. A crowbar is nothing when there's no suspicion. You and I may see hiding spots and risks of guns being found, but they don't know what we know." He gave Gray's leg a squeeze and stood up again. "They're most likely thinking it was left behind from some maintenance shit. So when you're not expecting to find anything, you won't look as hard. Okay?"

Gray gave another nod, and he mulled over what Darius had said. It made sense when he put it like that.

Darius left shortly after, and Gray didn't waste any time uncuffing himself. Jonas lifted his gaze and observed Gray as he slid farther down the bed and held up the key between his fingers.

"We can trust you, right?"

Jonas's expression didn't change. It stayed empty, and maybe a little curious. "I have an eight-year-old brother I have to get back to. He's on his own—or stuck in the system, I guess. I haven't seen him in over a year."

Good enough. There was no way to confirm anything out

here, and they didn't have the time to take any more steps back. Gray leaned forward and turned the key in the lock.

"Thanks. What do you need from me?" Jonas looked up at him with big light-brown eyes, and it tugged at Gray. They were close in age and body build, but there was an innocence about Jonas that had been tainted by horror. The guy had seen too much, and it showed.

"I don't know yet," Gray admitted. "Darius will fill you in about tomorrow when he comes back."

"Darius," Jonas replied softly to himself. He pulled up his knees and hugged them to his chest. "I'm still expecting this to go to shit."

"You and me both." Gray snorted and rounded the bed to check the fridge under the desk. Darius had saved some leftovers for them, and there was plenty of water and juice and snacks. "Are you hungry?"

"A little."

Gray grabbed what he could carry and returned to his side of the bed. "So, um…do you mind if I ask some questions?"

"Go for it." Jonas nodded in thanks and accepted a bag of chips, and it just wasn't good enough. Sensing his apprehension, Gray asked if it wouldn't be more comfortable to sit on the bed. Or if he'd like to sit at the desk; either way, he didn't want Jonas to sit on the floor.

Jonas cleared his throat and awkwardly got off the floor, then settled down on the bottom corner of the bed. It was as if he was afraid the bed was gonna bite him.

Actually…it was as if he didn't have any good memories from being in a bed lately.

"Darius won't lay a hand on you," Gray murmured. "You're safe here."

"He's been vicious with you." Jonas glanced at him hesitantly. "I was in the central den the night he bought you. I saw what he did."

Gray swallowed hard. "What he had to do," he corrected, gingerly feeling the scarred digits along the back of his neck. "He didn't have a choice. He has to make sure our cover isn't blown." The markings were healing slowly, though without infection. The same couldn't be said for the tattooed barcode, which reminded Gray to take his antibiotics.

"I hope that's true." Jonas stared at his lap and opened the bag of potato chips. "He's been watching me a lot, and I don't wanna be the next one who gets tortured to death."

Gray flinched, even as he registered the hint of dark humor, and managed a forced smile. "If I've learned one thing, it's that he's always planning the next strategy if one fails." He paused and opened a bottle of water. "Look, I have doubts too. I'm scared shitless to believe this might work. But if there's anyone who can get us out of here, it's him. *That*, I believe with all my heart."

Jonas nodded once and chewed slowly on a handful of chips. "Okay. Ask your questions."

Releasing a breath, Gray gathered his thoughts and went through the things Darius had told him. Mainly, he was interested in the organization's operations, how big it was, and what kind of trouble they could expect.

Hopefully, Jonas would have some intel.

"Do you know exactly how many are on board?" Gray asked first. "In terms of security, other staff, buyers..."

Jonas squinted at nothing and scratched his thigh. "I know there should be five buyers left, and one of them has a girlfriend or wife on board too." That had to be Charlie's owner. Which meant Linus's buyer had left with a woman too. "Security and staff... Those lines are blurrier. There are ten of us who—well... eight now. Who do the stuff I do. Bartend, serve dinner..." He trailed off and looked away for a moment, and Gray could fill in the rest of that sentence on his own. Jonas and the others on the waitstaff were disposable. "I'm not sure exactly how many guards there are—maybe nine or ten. Two of them are here against their will too."

Whoa. "Really?" That surprised Gray. "But they're armed. They can defend themselves."

Jonas lifted a shoulder. "Sometimes there's a gun pointed at someone they love, but for the most part, they owe the wrong people money. One way or another, there's a debt to pay off. It keeps them loyal."

Gray bit on a cuticle, wondering if this was gonna change things for Darius, who was always looking for weak links to expose. But trusting a guard…? Fuck, Gray couldn't imagine it. And they sure as hell didn't have the time to convince one of those dudes that everything would be fine if he helped them escape. Nor did Gray want to. He didn't fucking care if a guard was here because he was forced. No one forced the guards to rape and murder for kicks.

"This is a big crime organization, Gray. In the year I've been stuck here, I haven't seen a single slave make it out alive."

It put a rock in Gray's stomach, and for the first time, he wondered if they could ever be free. Even if they managed to escape, couldn't someone find them again? Holy shit, what if they went after parents and siblings?

"How did you get involved?" He pushed the words out before he went into a panic. He had a job to do, and Darius was counting on him. "You mentioned something about a job."

"I was already on the streets." Jonas seemed more casual now than before, the opposite of what Gray felt. "A buddy told me about some gig in Miami—this was back in Philly. But I had to go to them directly. I had to talk to someone in Texas. So that's where I went."

"Texas?"

Jonas nodded, reaching for a chocolate bar. "Human trafficking capital of the US. Dallas and Houston are fucking nuts. Tens of thousands of people come through there every year. It's a billion-dollar industry, and no one misses those girls. Who cares about a foreign girl? Nobody. Domestic ones get picked up when they're already trash. Runaways, prostitutes, users, you name it. Some dudes too, but..." He shrugged. "Anyway. I went down there and asked around until I found the right place. They were smart about it too," he told Gray. "They don't set off any warning bells by promising a bunch of shit. It was supposed to be quick cash for a temporary gig, and they needed a lot of guys. I knew before I got there that I'd probably be sharing a room with like, four other dudes. But it was work, and at the end of the summer, I was supposed to have enough to start a life for my brother and me."

Gray couldn't imagine. To walk into the trap like that, to realize you'd been set up, and then discovering there was no getting out. And Jonas had a kid brother somewhere who was on his own...? Jesus Christ.

"It was all right until we arrived in Miami," Jonas went on. "We'd had work training and knew our job was to look good in front of rich fuckers. And since then...I mean, since the first event took place out at sea, everything's been different."

"Have you tried to escape?" Gray asked quietly.

Jonas nodded jerkily, looking like he was struggling to stay calm. "Once. They managed to keep me in my place for a few months. I've thought about escaping every time we go back to Miami, but they said they were gonna kill my brother. So I didn't put up a fight for a while, and I was too scared. They—they did stuff to us, and I don't have to explain that to you. You already know."

Yeah, Gray knew.

"They keep us in an old motel outside the city," Jonas said. "The staff, I mean. They own the property, and we're never alone. Plus, we got these." He brushed his fingers over the back of his neck, and Gray instantly understood Jonas had been chipped like Charlie. "Anyway, I did try to run once, 'cause they made a mistake. I punched a guard, and I received the regular threats. They were gonna kill my brother and slit my throat and all that, but they also said they were watching my family. My whole family. And I don't have one. My folks are dead. So I thought I'd try to run the next time we docked, because it's closer to civilization, and I just needed to find a place to lay low long enough to remove the tracking device."

Gray caught himself right before he could ask if it worked. He was on pins and needles, his body tense, and he felt dumb as shit when he checked himself. Fucking obviously, it hadn't worked. Christ. The dude was here now, after all. But dammit, he needed some good news.

"I didn't get fifty feet before they were all over me." Jonas let out a shaky laugh, the pain growing tenfold in his expressive eyes. "I'd never felt as alone as I did that night. Not a single fucking person heard me scream." There was another chuckle, but Gray saw everything fall apart before it actually did. Jonas's shoulders shook, and then he covered his face with his hands and tried to hold back his sob. "I shouldn't have tried to escape."

Gray cursed under his breath and pushed away the food between them. Then he moved closer and cautiously put a hand on Jonas's shoulder. He went still for a second, an automatic response Gray had come to understand painfully well.

"Ask me the next question," Jonas croaked into his hands. "I don't wanna think about this anymore."

"All right. Um." Gray's hands fell to his lap, and he fidgeted with his fingers while he scrambled for the questions Darius wanted answered. "How many auctions have you been to?"

"Just auctions, or parties too?"

Gray didn't understand the question.

Jonas sniffled and wiped his face. "Parties are more common. Disgusting men bring their whores and slaves. Basically, it's a four-day-long play party, but instead of buying a slave, you bring one."

"Oh." Just when Gray thought the world couldn't get any uglier... "Both, I guess."

"There's something happening every month." Jonas cleared his throat and stared at his lap. "Parties usually have themes, and it's for...I don't know, I mean, they're still rich as fuck, but not as loaded as the men who attend auctions. Parties come with drugs, loud music, and business. They trade prostitutes, gamble, and network. There's a big drug trade, and a lot of guests come up from South America."

"Jesus." Gray rubbed his mouth absently, thinking how this whole clusterfuck just kept growing like a goddamn cancer.

"The auctions are more rare, especially one like this." Jonas gave the cabin a glance. "Last one was a couple months ago. Fourteen girls from Guatemala were sold to some creeps from Europe."

Gray didn't wanna hear another word. This organization operated all over the world, and the mere knowledge of it was throwing a dark shadow across everything he'd once found beautiful or appealing. What kid didn't dream about backpacking through Europe? If he went now, he'd wonder what restaurants, what hotels, and what checkpoints were used in trafficking networks.

Hell, he'd spent months in and out of trucks, riding on the same highways as anyone who was on their way to work. The entire goddamn world was nothing but a system of smuggling routes.

"What, uh..." Gray scrubbed at his mouth and jaw,

disgusted. But he had to move on. "What about this fleet of luxury boats? Are there a lot of them? Do you happen to know if we're in a heavily trafficked area?"

"I think...hmm. I think there are four yachts in total. They're not registered in Florida. They come here from Texas. At least, that's what I've overheard." Jonas paused. "There's another auction taking place somewhere around here now too. With the same theme, I mean. Gay guys. But otherwise, I haven't heard of two boats being out here at the same time."

That could be a good thing. Right? They weren't gonna want a bunch of boats nearby when they attempted to take control of this one tomorrow. Well, not boats that belonged to this vile organization.

He opened his mouth to ask the next question but promptly shut it again when he heard someone unlocking the door. Darius appeared, visibly tired, and closed the door behind him.

"Boys." He nodded with a dip of his chin.

"Hey." Gray took a deep breath, relieved to see him. "How did it go?" He noticed Jonas had become a lot more guarded.

Darius was noticing it too, and maybe that was why he made an effort to be as casual as possible. Although, Gray could see everything wasn't awesome. The pinch between Darius's brows was telling.

"Good news and bad," he admitted. He avoided that side of the bed, perhaps to give Jonas some space, and chose to sit down at the desk instead. "Bad news first. Three guards who're supposed to work tomorrow are already ill. I thought it was gonna be another few hours." He opened a window and dug out his cigarettes. "Unless my calculations are wrong again, the drugs will wear off too early, around noon instead of three or four." He rubbed his forefinger and middle finger along his eyebrows and grimaced. "Maybe if we start earlier too..."

"Do I even wanna know what was in that powder?" Jonas mumbled to Gray.

Gray's stomach was a mess of nerves, but for this, there was an ounce of humor to be spared. "I only know he crushed laxatives into the mix."

"You never know when an illness can come in handy," Darius had explained when he'd made the concoction. *"There's a reason we use it as our most common excuse to get out of things."*

Darius had brought it with him for the purpose of having an excuse in case Gray was too traumatized to play a part in their cover. The man really did try to think of everything.

"Okay, so what does this mean for the escape?" Jonas asked hesitantly. "Will it be harder to get away?"

Oh boy. He didn't know yet that they weren't running anywhere. Gray wet his lips and flicked his gaze to Darius.

He took a deep drag from his cigarette and exhaled the smoke toward the window. "No time to beat around the bush. We're not going anywhere, Jonas. We're going to take control of the yacht."

Ugh, it sounded fucking impossible when he said it out loud.

Jonas gaped at them both. "Are you two out of your fucking minds?"

"The good news better be really good," Gray told Darius.

His mouth twitched. "It is. I got the code to the pilothouse where the surveillance can be shut off."

Okay, that was...something, at least.

13

Despite having not gone to bed until after four in the morning, Gray woke up around seven.

He'd shared a bed with Darius for...three nights now. Yet, this felt like the first time. The stateroom's temperature was cool, almost a little chilly, and Gray pulled the duvet higher and shifted a bit closer to Darius. The man slept on his back, one hand under his head, the other resting on his stomach. The sun had reached his torso. Perhaps that was why he wasn't cold.

Darius's hair and scruff glinted in the morning light, and he was so fucking gorgeous. He looked more peaceful than Gray had ever seen, that was for sure.

It was such a different sight from last night. Or earlier this morning, technically. They'd showered after Jonas had been taken back to his quarters, and Darius had been all but dead on his feet coming out of the bathroom. And still, they'd stayed up and talked for-freaking-ever.

Today was going to be insane, and Gray didn't dare think that he might be free—actually free, in every sense—before the day was over. It was scary as hell, but he was ready to fight. So was Jonas.

"Darius," Gray whispered. "Darius, are you awake?"

He grunted sleepily and rolled onto his side. "No, Darius is asleep." He surprised Gray by pulling him flush against his body and drawing the covers over them.

Gray's breath hitched at the sudden onslaught of joy. Temporary as it was, he hadn't felt anything remotely close to happiness in months, but this did it. He was wrapped up in solid warmth that made him feel safe and protected.

"You realize we're cuddling, right?" Gray smiled to himself and scratched lightly at Darius's chest.

"Mm. Big fan." He hummed and ducked his head to burrow his face into the crook of Gray's neck. And *that* felt...even better. The soft rasp of his whiskers, the warmth of his lips. "Get some sleep, knucklehead."

"Uh, right..." Gray chuckled breathily and slipped one leg between Darius's. He cursed their underwear to the fiery pits of hell, too. "Kinda difficult to sleep when I'm in the arms of a man who's criminally fucking gorgeous."

Darius grew still, though he didn't tense up. If anything, the atmosphere was heavy with contentment. Next, he released a sigh and gave Gray's ear a little bite.

"I gotta admit something," he murmured drowsily. "You say shit I've never heard before."

"What do you mean?" Gray inched away and smiled curiously. "You can't tell me no one's told you you're hotter than sin before."

"Not the way you do it," he chuckled. "I didn't think last night was going to—fuck, now what?" Their conversation ended abruptly with the phone ringing.

Gray flipped onto his back and scowled at the ceiling while Darius rolled away to get the phone. He hadn't thought last night was going to what? Gray was gonna stew over this, he could feel it. Just like he did with all men he couldn't place into neat little categories. Oh God, maybe it was a self-destructive behavior. Did he attract the wrong men? Did he *get* attracted to the wrong men? History would indicate that. One man in denial, a couple closet cases, one who'd had more issues with his sexuality than Gray could handle.

And how does any of this matter now?

"What do you mean?" Darius spoke into the receiver and felt the need to get out of bed. "Is it contagious?"

Gray switched gears and sat up too. No, his stupid history with men meant absolutely fuck-all. There was a good chance he'd never have such a trivial problem again, so why bother thinking about it. Instead, he focused on Darius and the dreaded day they had ahead of them. Whoever was on the phone must've called because of the men getting sick.

"I see." Darius's expression turned grim, and he snapped his fingers and nodded for Gray to get up. "That's good. You can set an extra plate at breakfast for me." He wrapped up the call, and Gray stood on the other side of the bed, doing his best not to let the nerves get the best of him. "They're cutting the trip short because they can't be certain it's not food poisoning, so this is it. We gotta do this now."

"Oh God, we're gonna die." Gray clutched his stomach and felt his pulse skyrocketing. They weren't ready, they weren't ready. They hadn't gotten any chance to prepare Cole yet, and Jonas was still unarmed. They were supposed to have another few hours to work with!

"We are?" Darius stepped into a new pair of dress pants and lifted a brow at Gray.

"Well, maybe."

Darius snorted and got busy; the man could go from zero to sixty like a high-end sports car, not to mention how well he could multitask. While he buttoned up a crisp shirt, he also went over his notes that were spread out on the desk.

"You're ready for this, knucklehead." He didn't give Gray any room to argue. "Only two things will change, the time we begin and…this." He opened a briefcase, the one with a decreasing number of drugs. "It's human nature to be more alert and irritable when something's about to change, and today is the last day of vacation for these men. They have their journeys home on their minds, and this is both good and bad. Good because they're easily distracted, bad because they become harder to entertain." He pointed at Gray. "I need you to be the comic relief who lowers the pressure."

It dawned on Gray what this meant, and he nodded hesitantly. "You want me to act like I'm high as a kite."

"Yes. When we get upstairs for breakfast, I'm going to inject you with a placebo." Darius reached for the tie hanging over the desk chair. "It's important you know how heroin hits you. Have you ever taken opioids?"

Whoa, what the fuck? Gray folded his arms and grew defensive. "What do you take me for? I don't do drugs."

Darius didn't try to hide his amusement, though he stayed busy. "You're a hockey player, though. You get hurt all the time, and opioids are common in pain meds. I'm sure you're no stranger to Vicodin or oxycodone."

Oh. Well, no. Maybe he'd been on Vicodin once, after the time he got injured playing field hockey.

"Fine. I was prescribed Vicodin for a few days when I was seventeen. What about it?" Gray tried to unclench and ease the tension in his shoulders.

"I want you to remember the feeling it gave you." Darius paused what he was doing and gave Gray his full attention. "The pain fading, a calm washing over you. You probably felt sluggish. Maybe you laughed at nothing. Now, magnify that. Heroin takes hold quickly." He rounded the bed and grasped Gray by the shoulders, leveling him with a serious look. "You can't stop acting on this one, Gray. You have to keep pretending, no matter what you see and hear." He tapped Gray's temple. "It takes about thirty seconds for the drug to reach your brain stem, and once you're there, you gotta think about everything you do. Slow it all down. Your reactions—everything."

Gray blew out a breath and scrubbed at his face. *You can do this. You can pretend.* He did remember that time when he was seventeen, hazy as the memories were. He remembered his brothers having fun at his expense. He remembered the cotton mouth, the drowsiness, and the lazy grins.

"I nodded off and found random stuff funny when I was on those pain meds," he admitted.

Darius nodded. "Use that. Especially the nodding off. You'll be distracted by the euphoria in your body and weird thoughts."

Weird thoughts... Right. Gray raked his teeth over his bottom lip and nodded slowly. He would do his damnedest to pretend he wasn't bothered by the monsters he shared a table with. He'd slow down his reactions and drift off.

"Think you can sell it?" Darius tipped his head to hold Gray's gaze. "Think of it as a way to attract these men to watch you in the dungeon. The more you hold their attention, the likelier they are to show up for your punishment."

That made sense. If they got all ridiculous over seeing a crowbar, they probably had an urge to stay in their staterooms at the risk of a flu going around. But Gray and Darius needed as many as possible to show up in the dungeon after breakfast.

"I can do it," he said as confidently as he could.

"I know you can." Darius cupped the back of Gray's neck and pressed a kiss to his forehead. "Try to face the sun. It'll make your pupils smaller. We don't really have the time to fake any other outward signs of drug use."

Good lord, only Darius would think of something like that.

Before they left the stateroom, they freshened up and talked about what to do with Cole. Basically, they would have to make the best of the situation. If Gray came across a moment where he could warn Cole or give any indication of what was gonna happen, he would.

The good thing was that Cole was quick on his feet, and he was ready for anything. Gray felt in his gut he could trust Cole to seize any opportunity.

Cole wasn't on the upper deck. Only Lee and Oscar were restrained by the slave posts, and the breakfast table had seen more cheerful days too. The four men who sat there ate in silence, except for Vanya, who tried to make conversation. The blue-eyed psycho kid lit up when Darius took a seat, maybe hoping for a more interesting meal.

"Morning, gentlemen," Darius greeted.

There was a murmur of greeting in return.

When Gray ended up in the chair next to Darius, the joy in Vanya's eyes morphed into curiosity.

As per instructions, Gray had to give Darius a reason to inject him, so he slouched in his seat and reached for a muffin without asking.

Darius side-eyed him as he took a sip of coffee.

"You stare a lot," Gray told him.

It didn't take more than that to get everyone's attention.

"I see being lenient yesterday gave you back your voice." Darius set down his cup and retrieved the syringe from his pocket. "Let's see how much you'll add to your punishment now." He grasped Gray's wrist and gave his arm a swift tug, and Gray protested as Darius held the needle to his skin. "Stop fighting me, boy."

"Stop it!" Gray growled.

He winced, feeling the needle piercing his skin. The liquid

was injected, and Gray heaved a breath while the others mustered a few chuckles.

Vanya clapped. "Punishments are so much fun! Is there any chance you can do a public one, Mr. B? It saddens me that a few of our passengers are sick, and I think watching you with your toy would brighten everyone's mood."

Gray slumped back and feigned a violent body shudder. As Darius confirmed he had plans for Gray in the dungeon after breakfast, Gray turned his concentration on himself and went through the steps in order to look like he'd been injected with heroin.

The muffin fell from his hand, and he shook his head sluggishly. The most difficult part was the smile. Having to smile and act like he didn't have a care in the world broke his heart.

"I'll definitely stop by," one buyer said. He was the owner of Oscar and Lee, and Gray found it easier to grin when he thought of what he could do to the shithead. "My fuck-dogs spent the night in hysterics. I could barely sleep."

Motherfu—!

Gray took a deep breath and looked over at Oscar and Lee where they knelt. Beaten-up, stoic, defeated. Then he smiled, and he faced their monster of a buyer.

"You...you deserve to die," he said, only to let out a chuckle. "My tongue feels weird."

"Oh my." Vanya's gaze flickered with interest between Darius and Gray. Waiting for a reaction.

"You too," Gray told Vanya. He pointed unsteadily at the guy, remembering all the times he'd been drunk. How invincible he'd felt. "I wanna cut you open." He grinned lazily and planted his elbows on the table, his chin landing between his open palms. "You're such a deranged little shit. A psychopath. Are...are you even human?" He pressed on when he caught a glimpse of anger in Vanya's eyes. "Half human, maybe?" Gray snickered wildly and drummed his fingers along his cheeks. "I think your mom fucked a badger or something. And got preg-pregnant with you."

"Well." Darius wiped his mouth on a napkin, his interference allowing Vanya to relax. "You just earned yourself a ride on the mechanical bull, pet. And you know what?"

"*What?*" Gray smirked and rolled his eyes.

Darius nodded at the others. "*They* will decide when you're done."

Suffice to say, no one at the table was going to miss out on this.

"I hate that I have to put you through this."

"It was my choice." Gray bit off another strip of duct tape to attach the second knife around his calf. "None of the other implements in the dungeon would create a diversion as big as the bull, and you know it."

"I could've thought of something."

"No time for that now." Gray stood up from the bed and accepted the pair of loose sweatpants he'd wear. "I can handle pain." In fact, holding a pair of sweats gave him a more visceral reaction. He hadn't worn real clothes in months, and the soft fabric felt almost...luxurious. A part of him that'd been so dehumanized wondered if he was worthy.

"It's going to be a lot of pain, Gray," Darius pointed out patiently. "The spike mat will rip open your skin."

Gray tore his gaze from the black pants and stepped into them. "I can guarantee you I've been through worse." That didn't mean he wasn't glad Darius had advised him to protect his junk underneath the tight boxers. Hopefully, a thick sock wrapped around his dick would shield him in case he landed wrong.

Perhaps Darius could tell there was nothing to discuss. He nodded once and let it go. It was all business after that. They'd chosen the bathroom for their gun stash, because it wasn't the first place one's eyes landed when entering the suite, and it was in there Darius lined up their weapons. Gray stood in the doorway and eyed the counter as Darius checked the magazines to the three guns. If the cotton of the sweatpants didn't rub his skin so weirdly, Gray would've appreciated the moment more. Darius was a badass vision in a suit.

"Remember how to use it?" he murmured, attaching the magazine to one of the guns. "Only close range, count your bullets—"

"—and try not to waste them. I remember." Gray had been given a crash course in how to aim and fire one. The Glocks each had seventeen bullets, and Gray hoped with everything he was that he wouldn't miss too much.

He'd been instructed to lift the gun off of any guard he managed to take down, but he wasn't assertive enough to think that far ahead. He knew the plan, he knew his cues; aside from that, he was going to take it one step at a time.

"Good. Did you tape your hands?" Darius asked.

"Oh. No. I'll do it now." Gray pushed away from the doorframe and picked up the roll of duct tape again. Aside from having two blades taped to his right calf, he had the thin wire tucked into one of his pockets. In a battle between a neck and a couple fingers, the fingers would be severed. So he was wrapping the sturdy tape around his knuckles in order to use the wire in a fight.

The fight, he was ready for. Fuck, there was no word strong enough to describe how much rage and hatred he was ready to unleash on these murderers. The only thing that caused anxiety to prey on him from some dark corner of his mind was that people—innocent guys—could get hurt. Or worse.

With a big yacht like this, it was gonna be impossible to maintain the element of surprise for very long.

"When's Jonas joining us?" he asked.

"When you're down for the count, I'll go get him," Darius replied and exited the bathroom. "You'll be given a warning—loud enough for the others to hear. That by the time I come back with Jonas, you have to be seated on the machine again."

Gray nodded in understanding, though he was less chill on the inside now. This was really it. People were gonna die. Gray would likely be responsible for another person's death—or several. And he wasn't sure if he was supposed to feel bad about it. What if he couldn't—no. He could. End of fucking story.

Darius checked his watch. "All right, I think we've stalled enough. With a small dose, you'd be starting to come off the H now, so you can be a bit more lucid. And depressed."

Gray could do depressed. No problem.

After Darius had checked Gray's taped-up knuckles and once again reminded him to be careful and stay close once shit hit the fan, there was nothing to do but walk out of the stateroom one last time.

14

Darius had an arm around Gray's middle and was supporting him on the way down to the dungeon. The yacht was pretty quiet this late morning, and they only passed two men, one from the waitstaff, one guard.

Music greeted them in the dungeon, as did seven other motherfuckers. Oscar and Lee's owner was here alone, so was Philip—the British fuck who'd bought Cole—and then Vanya, three guards—Benny was one of them—and one guy who Gray had seen working alongside Jonas a couple times.

"There you are!" Vanya smiled widely and held out his arms.

"Remember." Darius pressed his lips to Gray's temple.

Gray remembered. Vanya couldn't die yet. Darius had deemed him valuable in case shit went south and they needed someone to bargain with. Gray didn't wanna think about that.

"I see you gave your toy some protection." Philip smirked and tipped his beer bottle at Gray's hands. Or maybe it was his sweatpants.

"So he'll last longer." Darius ushered Gray to the corner where the black, glossy mechanical bull waited. And the thin padded mat with plastic spikes that were about to break through Gray's skin in hundreds of places.

Gray took the first step onto the mat with caution, allowing his reactions to remain a bit slower than normal. He needed to stay calm. Calm and cranky. He grunted and shoved halfheartedly at Darius.

"I don't wanna do this," he said. "Fuckhead."

"Benny, go get my chocolate milk," Vanya demanded. "I don't want to miss a single second of this. Oh, and two lines."

Chairs were being pushed closer to the scening area, and Gray swallowed an onslaught of nerves as he hauled himself up on the bull with Darius's help. A bolt of panic followed when he noticed there was absolutely nowhere to hold on. The surface of the machine was too smooth to grip.

"I don't wanna do this," he repeated. Among the chuckles from the others, the tremor in his voice still sounded the loudest. To him, anyway. All he could do was lean forward and try to find purchase around the neck of the mechanical creature. "You wanted me to talk back to you!" He glared blearily, accusingly at Darius. "You asked for a rebel!"

Philip and Vanya laughed merrily.

Darius smiled and smacked Gray on the cheek. "Where's the rebel now?" With that said, he turned to the sick bastards. "Anyone care to make this interesting?"

Everyone cared. They placed bets on how many times Gray would fall off before he started begging.

I'm gonna kill you all.

"Son of a fuck!" Gray hit the spiked mat with a hoarse shout, and as the pain blazed through him, he tried to curl in on himself in a fetal position. The sharp spikes left his skin raw and bleeding, and the pain sucked all the air from him. Every time his body craved the relief of sobbing and weeping, all he could manage were choking sounds that rocked his upper body.

It was the third time the jerky movements of the bull had thrown him off.

Growing up with three rowdy brothers, how many times had he injured himself? How many times had his ass hit the ground and robbed him of breath? It was like that now, except the pain was coming from every angle, and little knives were turning him into ground beef.

Darius yanked him off the floor and hung him over the back of the bull. He checked for wounds that were too deep, but Gray croaked out another insult. A way of letting Darius know he could handle more.

"Stubborn kid," Darius muttered under his breath.

It was for the best, though. The assholes were having a good time; their defenses were lowered. They weren't thinking about going home, nor were they worried about the food poisoning.

As Darius pushed Gray's leg over the bull, he spoke for the others. "If he doesn't beg by the next drop, I have an idea." He wiped his bloodied hands on a tissue. "We give him a riding companion."

"Excellent!" Vanya cheered. The psychopath kid was high on cocaine and sipping chocolate milk through a straw.

One more drop... If Gray struggled to hold on before, it had nothing on now when he was bleeding from goddamn everywhere. Hands, arms, legs, and torso were smeared with blood, and a few smaller tears had appeared in his sweats.

His knees and shoulder blades suffered the most. It hurt like hell to land on them, but it inflicted the least amount of permanent damage. Okay, maybe not his knees, but there was no better alternative. His hip was in agony, he needed his feet so he could run later, and he had to take the weight off his calves where he risked exposing the knives.

His stomach flipped when the mechanical hell-ride started over. His hands were already slipping, and it became a game of trying to predict the movements and stay level on the bull. The shitheads laughed, the music droned on, the bets were upped, and salty tears stung and mingled with blood in the scrapes along Gray's cheeks.

Gritting his teeth, he squeezed his eyes shut and struggled against the violent movements beneath him. His muscles ached, and every effort made him sweat more. When shifting his head, he locked eyes with Darius, who sat in one of the chairs next to the others. But unlike them, he was tense. His hazel eyes burned with severity and barely restrained rage, reminding Gray of the flash of Darius's eyes he'd gotten the night he was auctioned.

"Forgive me."

The memory of the low whisper went through Gray like a breeze.

A second later, a rocky movement sent him flying off the machine. A somersault shot a bout of dizziness into him right before he squared his shoulders and landed on his back. *Ow...* The fire started up again. It was the first time he'd hit his head, and it hurt so much that he couldn't make a sound. He imploded instead, trapped by the consuming pain. He lost track of time and space. The agony was everywhere, blackening his vision, squeezing his lungs, and rendering his body useless.

We're not here. We're somewhere else. Just...me.

Something jostled him—or someone. Slippery hands felt his neck and forehead, and then he was airborne. *Darius...* Gray felt his lips form the name, but he heard nothing.

Shhh...

Gray took a shallow breath, one after another, and slowly came to his senses. Darius was lowering him into a chair.

"Snap out of it, boy." Darius gripped Gray's jaw and brushed his thumb over his bottom lip. "Get ready for the next game. We need to have our fun."

"The next game," Gray echoed in confusion. Fuck, this

amount of hurt was going to be impossible to forget. He blinked and focused on Darius. *The next game. Oh fuck.* "Yeah," he whispered. Suddenly fully aware he was surrounded by people watching them, he offered a small nod to let Darius know. *I'm with you. Next game.* Darius was going to get Jonas now.

This was it.

Darius snapped his fingers at a guard, a silent command for the fucker to follow. Gray memorized the man's stony expression, his high cheekbones, and his light hair. His perfectly straight nose and his dead eyes.

"I love that you don't beg," Vanya cooed. "Is it because you want to bring us more pleasure, hmm?"

Gray dragged his weary gaze from the door and fixed it on Vanya. How the hell could this slender little manchild be so fucking revolting? And downright terrifying. It was the angelic features masking the absolute purgatory of his mind that did it. Gray had never encountered anyone as evil as this guy. Because all Vanya wanted out of life was to make innocent people suffer. It made him happy. It lit up his baby-blue eyes with pure joy.

In too much pain to be sickened, Gray leaned forward and winced at the protests his joints made. His hands landed on his thighs, and he fisted the fabric in order to wipe the blood from his hands. He needed to get ready stat, and he wouldn't get far if the knives slipped out of his grip.

He wiggled his toes carefully. His feet had been spared, aside from a few scrapes. He didn't feel any blood underneath the soles, so that was good.

By now, Darius must've summoned someone to get Jonas, and then he'd come up with an excuse to stop by their cabin. "Just have to get something." Or whatever. Darius was creative. And once there, he'd get rid of any accompanying guard and grab guns before he and Jonas hurried to the second top deck.

Gray knew there were two scenarios, one of which would

leave him a sitting duck in here for a couple minutes. That was if Darius and Jonas encountered more people inside the pilothouse than expected. Then they might have to resort to using the guns, thus alerting everyone that something was wrong.

Gray braced himself for anything. His ears prickled, straining to hear anything above the music, and he pretended to stretch his back so he could feel his hands around his calves. His forehead almost touched his knees. *Deep breaths. Push back the pain.* His fingers played along the hems at the bottom of his pants.

He was ready to pull them up and access the blades. He was ready to rip the tape if the knives got stuck in their sheaths. He was ready to use the wire in his pocket. He was just so fucking ready.

He sniffled and wiped his chin on his shoulder. The bleeding was stopping in most places, thankfully. Only a few spots where the spikes had opened bigger wounds would need dressing later.

Where are they? Are they at the bridge yet? Have they shut off the cameras?

According to Jonas, there shouldn't be more than two people in there. Darius had dubbed them the background crew. They maneuvered the boat, they cooked, and one of them was close to Red, but they were rarely seen. They didn't show up for dinners or events.

Gray turned his head and rested his cheek on his knee, facing the door so he could see Darius and Jonas the moment they appeared.

Philip, seated on that side of Gray, looked down at him in amusement. "Is the toy sleepy?"

I'm gonna cut you first. I'm gonna stab you in the fucking throat.

Darius had warned Gray that it took more strength to cut through flesh than what the movies depicted.

"I wanted to buy you, I'll have you know," Philip went on. His British accent, Gray noticed, wasn't as pronounced when he thought of it. Maybe he lived in the US. "I always liked the boys who looked like they played college football."

No wonder he'd bought Cole, then.

Gray tightened his grip on the edge of his sweatpants.

Philip finished his beer and gave a dismissive wave. "Probably for the best Mr. B purchased you, though. I have enough work with my own heathen." He chuckled at something. "The way I made him scream last night... At long last, I should say. He's been hard to break." He winked at Gray. "The walls here must be truly soundproof. I'm surprised no one noticed."

Gray only offered a flat stare, and it didn't last long. He caught movement in the hallway and spotted Darius and Jonas walking toward them briskly. Gray sucked in a breath and felt a rush of adrenaline.

This is it, this is it. This is war.

"I'm back, gentlemen." Darius closed the door to the dungeon, something they hadn't done before, and smiled stiffly. To Gray, he nodded subtly as he gripped Jonas's neck. But rather than crossing the dungeon to where the others were waiting, they made a beeline for the two guards occupying a couch in the back.

"Yay, let the boys play for us!" Vanya clapped.

There would be no more playing. The game was over. Gray pulled up his sweats around his knees and gripped the two blades.

"No, he's mine," Jonas growled. "You will never rape me again, you fucking animal!"

Gray swiftly hauled out his knives, and he rammed the first one into Philip's neck. The man's eyes bulged out in shock, blood gushing around the blade that was now stuck. Gray shot up and witnessed the exact moment Jonas drove a knife into Benny's stomach. Darius worked faster and had already left the other guard in a heap on the floor.

It took a couple heartbeats for the dungeon to erupt into chaos.

With no time to waste, Gray faced the remaining men, and he saw Vanya and his panicked gaze. More than that, he was reaching for something, something he kept under that goddamn silk robe of his. *I don't fucking think so.* Gray didn't blink; he flew at the kid and unleashed the blinding rage he'd kept buried.

"I dare you!" Gray sent them tumbling back, the chair tipping over, and Vanya's scream pierced his eardrums. "I told you. I told you. I'm gonna end you all!" They hit the floor, and Gray got a grip on Vanya's throat. He pushed the little sadist down and opened his robe.

"Mom!" Vanya screamed. "Kill him! Ow!"

Gray grunted at the knee he got in his gut, and his hand shook. *Fuck. Get it together.* He saw the gun sticking up from Vanya's white silk pants, and he grabbed it with a trembling hand and pushed it away from them.

"Someone, get in here!" another man yelled.

"Can't breathe—" Vanya choked out.

Gray let out a growl at the pain and hauled the kid off the floor, only to slam him up against the nearest wall. He took in the fear in Vanya's eyes and smiled for the first time without wanting to hurl.

"You will die," Vanya rasped. "You won't get away."

Gray rammed his forehead forward, creating a perfect crunch at the impact with Vanya's nose. After that, the kid was a sobbing mess, and Gray let go of him. For now. Fucking bargaining chip… As he backed away, he caught Darius grabbing Lee and Oscar's owner. It was a euphoric and beastly sight.

A man who deserved to die. The same look of fear, the bulging eyes, face growing red, panic taking over.

Darius got his arm around the man's neck and twisted it hard, and though Gray couldn't hear it, he could practically feel the snap as the buyer's neck broke.

Gray looked around them and ran a hand through his hair. His body was buzzing, his hands wouldn't fucking stop shaking, and he waited for the anxiety to bubble up. His skin itched with the drying blood, but there was more than that. Foreign emotions were surging inside him, and he could only describe them as inhuman. His conscience had checked out.

"Get the gun, knucklehead."

Gray snapped out of his haze and blew out a shaky breath. Gun, gun—there. On the floor. The one Vanya had tried to use. Gray picked it up.

Hiding in a corner next to a couch was one of the guys from the staff. Shaking in fear. Jonas was trying to calm him down. *It's gonna be all right. We're getting out of here. We're going home.*

Gray swallowed hard and flicked a glance at Philip. Dead with his eyes open. Then Benny. Was he dead? Gray walked over and kneeled by his head—oh shit. He wasn't dead at all, though he certainly would be soon.

"Didn't I tell you?" Gray whispered. He eyed Benny's body. Jonas had stabbed him in multiple places. Darius must've taken his gun already, because his holster was empty. "You don't survive this. I only wish I could drag it out, because you deserve to suffer."

Benny's gaze was unfocused, and every time he tried to say something, he coughed up blood.

"Gray. We have to move on."

Gray gave Benny's cheek a smack and stood up to face Darius, who was tucking his tie into his pocket. Shit, he'd already restrained Vanya to the X-cross and taped his mouth. The psycho was barely moving, probably out of fear. Barbed wire circled the wood.

"Where do we go now?" Gray asked. "You said we have to set up a safe area and bring people there."

"Safe area?" Jonas questioned. He remained on the floor with the other guy. He'd stopped crying but was still upset.

Darius replied while folding up the sleeves of his button-down. "Since we're working with moving targets who don't know what's going on yet, we can't secure one deck and move on to the next." He nodded at the frightened boy. "We're gonna round up the staff in your quarters now, then go to the bridge. Jonas, you will stay there with them while Gray and I take care of the rest."

"I can do more than that." Jonas frowned.

Darius shook his head. "You'll have plenty to do, and we'll make sure you boys have means to defend yourselves if someone tries to enter."

"Anyone with the code can do that," Gray pointed out.

"The guards don't have it. Only Ms. Valerie and the crew," Jonas mumbled. "Okay, I'll keep watch. What about Ms. Valerie's son?"

"We can't bring him." It was the one thing Darius was grim about. "Gray and I will come back for him later."

Then they better hope no one came in here and rescued him first. Gray understood, though. Vanya wouldn't cooperate for shit, and they'd get themselves killed if they had to lug him around all while facing gunshots from others.

15

According to Jonas, there were only two other guards on duty right now, so after closing the door to the dungeon, they made their way down the hall that led to the aft of the yacht.

Gray felt naked, wanting to keep his gun aimed in case they ran into a guard. But Darius reminded him they were more likely to cause destruction if they waved their guns around for no reason. And to the guards and the others on the boat, it was still "no reason." For all they knew, Darius was Gray's owner and everything was peachy.

Darius's line of thinking gave Jonas an idea.

"Stay back when we get to our quarters," he murmured as they passed the central den. Gray studiously faced forward. He didn't want to see the space where he'd lost his freedom for money. And he'd been one of the lucky ones... *Jesus Christ, stay focused.* He tuned in to what Jonas was saying. "...won't bat an eye if I tell them Ms. Valerie wants to see them."

Darius acknowledged him with a nod and stopped as they reached a staircase. He peered up and down the stairs, then gestured for them to follow him up. Gray grew antsier and antsier, and he glanced over his shoulder. The boy clinging to Jonas was about to cry again—*shit*. Gray stumbled, having walked straight into Darius.

"Just the man I was looking for," Darius said, and a beat later, a guard appeared around the corner.

Holy shit, Gray's heart was pounding.

"What can I do for you, sir?" The guard acted completely normal, though he took on a mildly curious expression at the sight of Jonas and the other guy. Gray and the blood he was covered in, however, got a smirk and a once-over.

Die.

"Right here—I have a problem." Darius coaxed the guard down a few steps on the stairs so they were out of sight. And before Gray could even blink, Darius had his tie around the guard's neck, and he was choking the fucker out.

Gray jumped into action instinctively and covered the mouth and nose of the guard. If it didn't speed things up, at least it would muffle any noises. Darius clearly didn't need any help handling the man's violent thrashing. He stood rock solid, even as the guard tried to kick himself free.

"Shh, it's okay." Jonas had to comfort the other guy. "Just follow my lead, all right? We're going home, Rob."

"You can't use that name," the guy—Rob—whispered in panic. "We don't have names."

Gray cursed at what he'd overheard, and anger took over for a moment when he slammed his elbow against the guard's temple. And it fucking worked. The last strength to struggle ran out of him like water, and Darius snorted in amusement.

"All right, cover for me," he murmured. "We need to hide him."

Gray went ahead to make sure the coast was clear, and he nodded as all he saw was an empty hall—in both directions. Then he jerked back a step and went a little wide-eyed. Darius wasn't fucking around, was he? He grunted and hauled the guard over his shoulder. If he thought the body was unbearably heavy, it didn't show.

In a supply closet across the hall, Gray helped him dispose of the guard, and Darius earned himself another gun.

He tucked it into his pants at the base of his spine. "Okay, that's four guards down. One more to go who's working right now. Be on the lookout, boys."

Boys... Gray let Jonas and Rob go before him this time so he could cover their backs. He didn't know why, but he wanted to be Darius's equal for this. The others could be the "boys," and Gray would just be Gray. Even though he was the same age as them.

The path to the staff's quarters was short and uneventful, only serving to build more tension in Gray's body. He never stopped looking over his shoulder; he just waited for shit to hit the fan.

Gray and Darius stayed in the background as Jonas opened the door to their room. He spoke in the monotone voice Gray recognized from when Jonas had brought Darius sunscreen.

"Ms. Valerie" wanted to see everyone right away outside the pilothouse, and it was as painful as it was comical how quickly the guys got ready. The small cabin had bunk beds taking up each wall, and it took the five guys less than a minute to put on new underwear and smooth down their hair. No room for modesty or privacy when they didn't even have their freedom. Yet.

"Where's Owen?" Jonas asked.

"Pool deck, I think," another one answered.

Gray exchanged a look with Darius. They'd have to go up there and find the boy.

Maybe the guys had been pushed down and abused to the point where they'd stopped being curious, maybe they'd been instructed never to question anything...maybe a combination of both. Either way, they didn't look remotely interested in knowing why Darius and Gray were out in the hallway, and other than offering Darius a slightly more polite expression, nothing gave away their thoughts. Jonas and Darius took the lead, and Gray stayed back once again.

This time, Gray didn't care about pretenses. He had a firm grip on the gun sticking out of his pocket, and he was ready to use it.

The peace and quiet was starting to seriously bother him. Granted, he knew several people were recuperating from being sick all morning, but this was crazy. It seemed the entire deck was empty.

"Hey," Gray whispered. At anyone, he reckoned. "Do you know if there's anything going on by the pool?"

There was only silence until Jonas gave them an expectant look and murmured, "It's okay. You can speak to him."

That caused more confusion between the boys than anything else. Christ, Darius was right. How on earth would anyone go back to any semblance of normal after something like this?

"Um, Owen's probably serving," one boy replied quietly. "Nikolaj and I helped Federico make soup for those who've been sick. I don't know if there's anything else."

Okay. Okay. That made sense. Gray released a breath and glanced over his shoulder. They were almost at the front of the yacht again, and now he only hoped none of the doors they'd passed opened just yet.

"What is going on?" one boy asked under his breath. The first one to show any curiosity.

"I'll tell you soon," Jonas whispered back.

"Hey, where do you boys think—sir? What's going on here?"

Gray's heart jumped up into his throat at the sound of the man's voice behind him, and he instinctively drew the Glock as he spun around. *Shit, shit, shit.* This wasn't the close-range

Darius had told him about. The guard was at least forty feet away, and Gray wasn't sure he could aim that well.

"Whoa, what the—" The guard pushed open his suit jacket, revealing a holster, and Gray didn't think.

He fired. With his fucking eyes closed. Amidst a burst of shock from the staff guys, from shrieks to cries, the sharp sound from the gunshot caused Gray to stumble back and flinch. His ears popped and started ringing loudly, and he ducked as someone pushed past him.

Another shot was fired. Gray sucked in a breath and forced his eyes to open, and it was Darius—of fucking course—who stood next to him with his gun raised. Way down the hall, the guard had dropped to the ground, and blood was pooling around his head, turning the beige carpet red.

Holy fuck.

"Everyone on the boat heard that. Let's go." Darius grabbed Gray's arm and shoved him forward. "You okay?"

Gray jerked a nod, his ears still ringing. He hadn't expected it to be so loud, nor had he anticipated the force traveling up his arm from firing a gun. "I fucked up," he said, and he hated himself for it. So far, he hadn't been of any use at all. "I'll do better." He locked and unlocked his jaw to release the pressure in his ears.

"I don't see how that could've ended any differently." Darius gave Gray's neck a quick squeeze, then let go to usher forward two staff boys who were close to hysterics. "We're almost there, but we gotta hurry."

He was right. The jig was up, and there would be no more sneaking around now that the first shot had been fired. Jonas could comfort his friends later; right now, they had to get to the pilothouse. So Gray helped Darius move the boys toward the end of the hallway, all while looking behind him even more often.

Darius stopped short right before the corner and cursed. Was someone coming? There was another set of stairs, Gray knew. The bridge was up there. Before he could ask, Darius pushed away from the wall, raised his gun, and rounded the corner. It was instantly followed by two shots and two thumps.

Gray strained to hear past the chaos and thought he heard tumbling, as if someone was falling down the stairs.

"Okay, let's go." Darius had lost the last shred of patience in his voice, and he crossed the hall, ushered everyone up the last set of stairs, and punched in the code to enter the pilothouse. Once the door was open, he gave the area a quick scan. "Get in, boys. Jonas, you're in charge." He stepped aside so everyone could get inside, and he held out an extra gun to Jonas. "You only give this to someone you can count on." Next, he nodded at Gray. "Knucklehead, give him the wire."

So much for needing to have his knuckles taped. It hadn't helped much on the bull either.

Gray retrieved it from his pocket and handed it over to Jonas. Being in the middle of the hallway gave him a full view of two bodies in the stairwell.

In the meantime, Darius extended his tie too, as well as a knife. "We'll be back soon, and only open that door if you hear a double-tap knocking. We clear?"

Jonas nodded jerkily, nervous but ready to fight for his life. It was a look Gray would forever recognize after this.

If they survived.

Gray had no recollection of the bottom deck of the yacht. It was narrower and more cramped, but no less upscale. The guards had two cabins, one down here, which turned out to be empty. Gray and Darius had picked up speed and were running down the hall, up the stairs, and kept running until Gray was shoved back.

"Quiet." Darius took a breath and put himself between Gray and the corner, where they heard voices.

"It's hard when we don't know who to look for," someone said with a sneer in his tone. There was an accent too—vaguely Latin American. "I never trusted that piece of shit from Texas, though. He's been hanging around the kitchen. Were you there when his luggage went through inspection? He brought enough equipment to kill all the slaves four times over."

Oh God. Gray pressed himself to the wall and forced himself to breathe steadily. The Texan, or Mr. K, was Milo's buyer. Nothing slashed through Gray as painfully as knowing that sweet kid had ended up with one of the worst men on board. Gray could still hear Milo's sobbing pleas and see how he shook in terror.

"I don't think so," another man replied. "At drinks the other day...he bragged too much about how cruel he is. The most vicious son of a bitch won't say a word. I bet it's the one in Twelve. Mr. B."

Gray raised a brow at Darius, who didn't move a single muscle. He was too focused—

"Guys!" That was someone else, someone farther away. "Valerie needs help!"

Once again, Gray turned to Darius, but there was nothing. Not until the sounds from the two men were fading, their feet rapidly running up the stairs. Then Darius jerked his chin in the same direction, and they followed.

"Where are we going?" Gray asked, out of breath. "We should be hiding Vanya somewhere else."

"No time. Up here." Darius took aim as they headed up another level, and Gray realized they were heading for the staterooms where Cole, Oscar, and Lee were.

At least it should be easy to rescue them. Their owners were already dead. Milo and Charlie were another matter. They were below them, a bit closer to the center of the yacht, if Gray had counted the numbered doors right.

Darius stopped outside Cole's cabin. "Listen to me carefully now." He leveled Gray with a grim look. "Unless the boys are restrained in a way that you need my help, I'm gonna leave this to you. I have to go get Charlie and Milo downstairs because their buyers should be feeling better now. The last thing we want is for them to give more resistance."

"I understand." Gray nodded quickly.

Darius pointed his gun at the lock on the door. "Once you're alone, you'll only have a minute or so. They'll hear the gunfire."

It was okay. Gray had gotten his shit together, and his mind started racing to think of complications. He'd free Cole first and — "I need an extra gun. Cole will help out."

"Unless he's too injured." Darius wasted no time and fired at the lock, causing the door to rattle. Then he rammed his shoulder against the door, without much happening. "Fuck." He glared and took aim at the hinges instead. Gray plugged his ears and flinched at the piercing sounds, but it was worth it. The door flew open, and Gray darted inside to find Cole naked, restrained, and gagged on the bed.

Darius surveyed the room, handed an extra gun over to Gray, and said he'd get the other door.

Gray didn't waste any time. He shoved the glimpses he got of torture devices on the desk out of his mind and hurried over to the bed. Cole's wide eyes full of frenzy, unshed tears, and hope became etched into Gray's goddamn retinas.

He spoke with his voice thick from a sudden onslaught of emotion. "Sorry it took so long. We're improvising a bit." He folded Cole's hand forward as much as he could and directed the gun at the shackle. Cole jumped at the gunfire, and Gray got one hand free.

On the other side of the bed, he did the same, aiming at the chain by the lock mechanism.

There was a sharp rap on the doorframe; it was Darius. "You're on your own. Lee and Oscar will be fine. Meet me by the stairs on this floor when you're done."

"We'll hurry." Gray refocused on Cole, who was tearing off the ball gag strapped around his head.

"*Fuck...*" Cole heaved a breath and pulled his hands to him. "I thought the whole thing was off."

Gray shook his head and glanced around quickly for something Cole could wear. "Are you okay to fight if it comes to—"

"For my fucking life, man." Cole grunted and got rid of the spreader bar between his ankles.

"It's loaded. Just pull the trigger if you see someone." Gray put the second gun on the mattress for Cole and picked up a pair of discarded boxer briefs off the floor. "I'll go help Lee and Oscar."

Entering the next room, he encountered both the others in the process of untying the rope that'd restrained them together. Darius must've freed their hands before taking off. Lee was worse off than Oscar, though neither had been spared abuse. Gray worried about the noticeable limp that Lee—*shit*. Gray ducked automatically at the sound of gunfire; he'd never fucking get used to it. Three rapid shots. It better be Darius who was freeing Charlie and Milo. There was a wife or something to kill too, wasn't there? Another double shot.

How many owners were still—

"What's happening?" Oscar asked shakily. "That guy—your owner. He told us to listen to you."

"We're taking back our freedom." Gray helped rid them of the rope and wiped his forehead with the back of his hand.

Sweat and blood were smeared all over him, and he had to look like a complete psycho. "Stay behind Cole and me, okay? We'll explain everything."

Soon it was the four of them out in the hallway, with Gray taking the lead and Cole covering their backs, and they moved hurriedly toward the stairs. Darius was on his way too; Gray spotted him coming up the stairs with Milo thrown over his shoulder and Charlie limping and clinging to Darius's free arm.

Gray told the others to stay put, then ran toward Darius to help out.

"Are we really going home?" Charlie croaked. The frenzy in his stricken gaze was getting too fucking familiar for Gray, who merely nodded and let the guy lean on him instead.

"G-Gray?" The hoarse whisper came from Milo. "Is that you? I'm s-scared."

"I'm here, Milo. You're safe now." Gray wasn't sure the boy had heard him. As they headed closer to the stairs, he walked slightly behind Darius, and he carefully pushed some hair away from Milo's face. His eyes remained swollen shut, and the dried blood around his ears spoke of repeated abuse with a vicious purpose.

Milo whimpered at the light touch, and Gray removed his hand, unsure. He didn't know just how traumatized Milo had been, but he guessed a whole fucking lot.

Upon reaching the stairs, Darius told everyone they were going to the pilothouse. Cole insisted on helping him and Gray, and Darius didn't say no. They did need the assistance, because at this point it was a round of hide-and-seek. Red and the few guards who were left could be anywhere, and then there was the matter of Vanya.

A gunshot rang out somewhere above them, causing Charlie and Milo to cry out, and Darius cursed. As if this wasn't bad enough, the gunfire was followed by someone screaming, "I'm going to fucking murder you!" and Gray would know that voice anywhere. Vanya had been freed.

"Darius," Gray whispered urgently.

"I'm thinking," he snapped under his breath. "All right. Counting high, can't be more than five guards left, including remaining crew. Only one guest left aside from me—Milo's owner."

"Red and Vanya," Gray added quietly.

Darius nodded with a dip of his chin and lowered Milo to the floor. "Boys, I need you to help him. Stay behind us." He was looking at Lee and Oscar. "Cole, Gray, I need you both ready. Chances are they're trying to get into the bridge, and if we lose that area, they can contact the mainland." He paused, eyeing Cole. "You ever fire a gun before, son?"

Cole nodded. "Yes, sir. Grew up on a ranch."

"Then don't point it at your feet. Let's go."

Gray's mouth twitched, and he took in Cole's chagrined scowl with a pinch of amusement. It was about as much fun as they had time for, and shortly after, they were moving again. Swiftly and silently up the stairs, three guns took the lead with Darius's in the middle, and Lee, Oscar, and Charlie followed with Milo.

The closer they got to the front of the yacht, the more commotion they heard.

"Just shoot the damn lock!" It was Vanya again.

"Won't help much when they've blocked the door, sir," someone else bit out. "It's already unlocked."

Go, Jonas, Gray thought. But whatever they had blocked the door with wouldn't hold forever. Not with how the guard kept ramming into it, each thump growing louder.

Gray threw a glance over his shoulder to make sure they had no one following them, and he almost missed Darius's signal. Gray frowned. Darius was insistent; he repeated the signal for two targets, then looked at Gray's gun with a shake of his head. The stubborn bastard was going to handle this on his own because he *still* didn't want Vanya dead.

Gray trusted Darius, though, and when they were close enough, he did nothing. He watched Darius take down the guard with a quick bullet before he grabbed Vanya by his throat and smashed him up against the wall.

"Where's your mother, boy?" Darius growled.

Vanya choked and spluttered, clawing fruitlessly at Darius's hands and arms.

There was a faint sound behind them, and—

"Gray!" Charlie cried.

"Release my son, Mr. B."

Gray went rigid at Red's voice. The gun in his hand trembled. Holy fuck, had they been ambushed? The hall had been clear! Unless—*fuck*. Gray turned slowly, and his face drained of color. Red wasn't alone. She and another two guards stood there, and they had guns pointed at Charlie, Milo, and Lee.

Red forced Charlie down on his knees and bumped the end of her gun against his head.

A door a few feet away was open. Maybe it was another cabin; either way, they'd probably come from there. Gray had fucking missed it.

"You can't win this one, Valerie," Darius said grimly. "We've already taken care of everyone else."

Red barked out a loud laugh. "If only you knew how wrong you are." A sickening smile played on her lips as her gaze traveled between the boys. It landed on Gray. "When your precious savior is dead, I'm going to sell your fucking body parts."

Gray lifted his gun and tried not to let his hand wobble. So much could go wrong here, and fear spiked like it never had before. He did his best not to show the terror, but he wasn't sure he managed. Red didn't look afraid with a gun aimed at her.

"Gray?" Milo sniffled. He was trying to open his eyes without any success. "What's going on?"

"Put your gun down, Valerie," Darius ordered. "If you—"

"Do you think I'm playing a game?" Red shrieked. A second later, her gun was directed at Milo, and a loud shot exploded in the hallway.

Gray's eyes widened in horror, and it was as if the whole world slowed down. He registered every fraction of a second. Milo's expression, frozen in fright and confusion. His body sagging forward until he landed face first with a muted thud. Blood gushing out of the wound at the back of his skull.

Dead.

Dead.

She killed him.

Tears and rage flooded Gray's eyes, and he refocused on Red. He pulled the trigger once. Twice. Three, four, five fucking times. He shot her over and over, and he cursed, and he screamed, and he flew into her so they tumbled to the floor. More shots rang out. Chaos erupted. Gray didn't give a fuck. He only saw this ugly fucking creature, and he kept emptying his gun. He shot her in the stomach, in the shoulder, in the neck, several times in her face. *Click, click, click.* His hand trembled, his vision was too blurry, his chest heaved. Gun empty. He punched her instead. He smashed his fists into her bloody mess of a head, he lifted it and crushed it against the carpet, and he screamed out the pain.

Fuck, he couldn't breathe. The hurt was eating him alive. She'd killed him... Milo was gone. That sweet fucking kid, dead for nothing. Dead because of these sick *monsters*.

He was just a kid.

The pain spread in sharp pulses and became one with his rapid heartbeat. It was the only thing Gray heard. He *heard* the agony, was consumed by it, and he barely registered that someone was pulling him away.

"He was just a kid…" The strangled sob that escaped his throat didn't sound like him.

Gray, Gray, Gray, knucklehead. "Gray." A growl pierced through the thick fog. "Snap the fuck out of it. I need you."

Gray buried his face in his hands, unable to stop crying, unable to stop the murderous hatred, unable to stop his chest from cracking wide open. *Snap out of it. Darius needs you. He needs you.* Gray tried. He fucking tried, but the grief was crippling. If only one innocent guy had been able to walk away from this, he would've wanted it to be Milo.

"Knucklehead, *listen* to me. It's not over yet. We have to secure the boat."

Secure the…fuck, because there were others. Another surge of wrath took hold of Gray, but this time, it pushed him forward. He shoved at the arms that had him in a protective cage, and he flew up from the floor to survey the hallway. Blood…fucking everywhere. Two guards down—dead. Vanya—dead. Cole was kneeling over Milo's body, crying silently and wiping blood from the boy's face.

Lee and Oscar were trying to comfort Charlie.

"Come here." Darius filled Gray's field of vision and had a tie in his hands. Hadn't he given that to Jonas…? "Can you focus?"

Gray nodded dumbly and side-eyed the dead guards. And Red was…unrecognizable. *Wait.* One of the guards no longer had a tie around his neck, and then Darius was down on one knee before Gray, tying the black silk around his thigh.

Gray hissed at a sudden burst of fiery pain. "What're you doing?" he rasped.

"You caught a stray bullet when you dove."

Oh. "It doesn't feel that bad."

"It will." Darius finished the temporary solution—to limit the bleeding, Gray realized. "We'll get the bullet out and dress it later. Right now, we have company. Think you can suck it up?"

"Dick," Gray whispered under his breath. "Yeah, I'm with you. What company?"

Darius rose from the floor and sent the ceiling a glance. "Helicopter."

Gray wiped the tears from his face and tried to hear anything, but his ears wouldn't have it. There was an underlying ringing sound and the wash of the ocean; that was it.

Darius turned to Cole. "You up for it, kid?"

Before Cole could answer, two gunshots blasted through the air outside. Darius narrowed his eyes at the ceiling, and Gray's heart jumped up in his throat. At least it plugged the grief temporarily, and he could think again.

"Who's shooting?" he croaked. "Shit—there's that guy from the staff. Owen? Are they hurting him?" Fuck if Gray knew, but he wouldn't put it past whoever was still alive. A guard or two, the owner from Texas...

"No, I don't think so, but we gotta go." Darius handed Gray a new gun, and Cole still had his. Before they went anywhere, Darius double-knocked on the door to the pilothouse and told Jonas to open. Then he instructed Charlie, Lee, and Oscar to hide out with the staff.

On the way to the stairs, Gray inspected his new gun, sure this one felt lighter. It'd belonged to a guard. And right then, he heard something. Had Darius been right? Was there a helicopter nearby? It was getting closer. A juddering *thump-thump-thump-thump* of the blades had Darius taking three steps at a time before he came to an abrupt stop in the little alcove at the landing. On the other side of the glass door was the upper deck, and they didn't know what they were facing.

"You boys stay behind me," Darius commanded quietly. He

was looking out the glass, maybe trying to spot the helicopter. He barely fucking flinched when another shot was fired, this one cracking like thunder.

Someone screamed somewhere on the deck.

Darius rubbed a hand over his jaw. "It's starting to look a lot like friendly fire."

That was...*good*? Right?

The helicopter had to be over them, or really close, when Darius carefully opened the door and peered outside. Gray was right there with him, and he watched as a black chopper came into view on their port side. A man was visible in the back, where it was completely open, and he was attaching something to his waist and making a rapid circular motion to the pilot. However the pilot responded, the other man gave a thumbs-up and picked up a bundle of rope.

When Gray caught the man's profile, there was no missing the rifle on his back. Even against the army green of his body-hugging T-shirt, the black weapon that looked like it belonged in a war zone stood out like a sore thumb. It screamed of danger, and Gray inched toward to Darius. Who was...smirking?

"Angel's gonna fucking kill me," he murmured.

"Who?" Gray frowned.

"My brother's wife." Darius opened the door wider and stepped out onto the deck as the chopper hovered closer. The rope was dropped and landed near the pool. "And *that*...is Ryan."

16

But...what? That hadn't been the plan, had it? His brother wasn't supposed to be here now.

Ryan was out of the helicopter, lowering himself to the yacht like he'd done it a million times before. Gray knew about his military background, so perhaps he had. He had the same badass fuck-off vibe that Darius had, and they were built similarly. Broad shoulders, muscular arms and thighs, solid frames, without looking too cut. It was strength that'd been built over years and years of service.

"You felt now was the time to bring in the cavalry? When we're done?" Darius walked toward his brother, and he tucked his gun into his pants at the base of his spine.

Ryan landed with a thump and signaled something to the chopper. Then he wiped a hand over his mouth before it stretched into a grin. "Didn't I just take care of three men for you? I'm pretty fucking sure I did."

Gray stayed back with Cole, who looked confused.

"Darius's brother," Gray explained quietly. "He's been helping out."

"Oh." Cole squinted into the sunlight as the helicopter left.

"What the hell are you even doing here?" Darius clapped Ryan on the cheek and pulled him in for a hug. "How did you know it was safe?"

"Squeezy got into the surveillance system, so she alerted me when everything went dark. You've also been way off course for the past hour. I'm guessing autopilot." Ryan wrapped up the hug with a smack to the back of Darius's head. "You can't stick to a goddamn plan, can you?"

"Gray's like Lias. He has to save the strays." Darius rubbed the back of his head while Ryan glanced over at Gray with amusement in his eyes. They were bluer than Darius's hazel ones.

"Good quality. Nice to see you alive, son," Ryan said with a nod at Gray. "Your family's waiting for you back in Miami."

Mom...? Gray swallowed hard. The whole thing was bizarre. There was no way, was there? Like...was it *over*? Incomprehensible. Actually, he refused to believe it. Mom and his brothers existed in another world, one that was nothing like this hell. Here, people died. Here, Milo was shot in the head for no motherfucking reason other than Red wanting to show she was serious. Here, Linus was used for target practice before his body was lost in the ocean forever.

"Why are you here?" Darius refocused and grew serious.

Ryan followed suit. "There's a storm brewing according to Squeezy, but we can talk about that later. The vessel secure yet?"

"I have to do a last check," Darius answered. "Literal storm or figurative?"

"The latter, I'm afraid." Ryan nodded at the pool. "There's a kid hiding behind that stack of chairs, by the way. He didn't look like a target to me."

That had to be Owen, the guy from the staff.

"All right. You and I can round up the bodies and make sure it's clear," Darius said. They were heading over to where Gray and Cole stood like statues, and Darius addressed Gray next.

"Knucklehead, you can bring everyone up here. Once Ry and I are done, there are wounds to dress."

"Um, okay."

An hour later, the upper deck was like a hospital. Jonas and a guy named Nikolaj from the staff were running between the loungers to take care of those who couldn't cope as well. Whether they needed comfort and help to understand what was going on, or they had physical wounds that needed tending to, Jonas and Nikolaj were there.

Gray and the guys he'd been brought here with had ended up at the dining table instead, and it was Cole who still had the energy to take care of others. Gray had run out of steam after explaining the whole purpose of Darius being here and how everything had gone down.

Physical pain hit Gray in waves, in a way it hadn't before. To anyone else, he probably looked relaxed in his seat, feet perched on the table, but on the inside, he was in fucking agony. He couldn't move.

Charlie came first, though. He was across the table from Gray, and he had his forehead touching the table while Darius held him still so Ryan could remove the GPS chip. Charlie wept continuously, his trembling fingers digging into the linen cloth.

"They didn't think this shit through," Ryan muttered. Brow furrowed in concentration, scalpel slicing into the flesh of Charlie's neck. "You wanna give it a try?"

Darius shook his head and gave Charlie's shoulder a soft squeeze. "Your hand is steadier than mine." He paused. "Charlie, you think you can hold still without me holding you? I need to get the bullet out of Gray's leg before he loses too much blood."

"I-I won't m-move," Charlie whimpered.

Gray averted his gaze to his lap and breathed through a thick rush of grief. It seemed every whimper was going to remind him of Milo and how he'd sounded. *Fuck*...he wasn't supposed to be dead. And he'd been from Camassia too. He'd been almost the same age as Gray's twin brothers. What if they'd gone to the same school? What if they'd been friends?

"Why didn't you call the police?" There was a pause before people glanced at Cole, who'd asked the question. "You knew we were here when you boarded. You knew we could die."

Darius cleared his throat and straightened after gathering some medical supplies off the table. "I didn't know for sure that Gray was on this boat until I saw him. I couldn't risk anything on an educated guess."

It wasn't the first question any of the guys had asked, and it wouldn't be the last. Gray was torn between wanting to defend Darius and...well, doing nothing. Because in the end, he understood everyone was mindfucked and wanted to know. The months leading up to this voyage from hell had been bad enough, but they paled in comparison. Lives had been lost, hearts had been broken, spirits had been crushed.

It didn't feel like it was truly over, either. The yacht had been searched, weapons had been collected, and the bodies of the vile creatures had been locked inside the dungeon. They were all dead, yet Gray was on pins and needles for the next blow.

He could tell there was *something*. He could see it in Darius's calculating expression. And who could forget what Ryan had said about a storm brewing.

Darius rounded the table and pulled out a chair. He didn't speak or make eye contact, working as if no one was around. He carefully shifted Gray's feet off the table and his injured leg onto the chair, where he placed the medical supplies too. Gray had stripped off his sweats as instructed earlier, and he'd pulled up his boxer briefs a bit so they weren't in the way.

"I'm afraid all I got is lidocaine and alcohol," Darius told him. "What will it be?"

Gray lifted a shoulder and stared at the gunshot wound. It wasn't bleeding as badly as it had, and other pains won out at the moment. Either way, he didn't give a flying fuck. Everything was gonna hurt regardless.

Darius sighed and poured something onto a piece of cotton and began cleaning the area around the wound. Gray hissed at the sting but was more worried about the actual procedure of removing the bullet. Maybe he should think again on the alcohol...

"It doesn't feel like everything's over," he said instead, keeping his voice down. "You have that look on your face. You've been different since you got back with your brother."

Had they found something on the boat, or was Ryan's news that shitty?

Darius flicked a glance at the guys around the table and decided to relocate the conversation. He told Gray to stand up and not put any pressure on his leg, after which Darius moved the two chairs closer to the aft railing. It gave them some privacy to talk, and Gray was relieved not to be treated like the others.

"I should've known Ry was gonna stay close," Darius admitted. "More than that, I should've known our sister wasn't gonna be able to stop digging." He inspected the wound in Gray's thigh with a frown of concentration, his fingers ghosting over the area he'd cleaned. "Long story short, it looks like my original plan to get you away would've been a bust anyway. Squeezy—that's Willow, our sister—she found out these trips are for more than hosting auctions. They're for drug trade too."

Gray bit his lip to keep from screaming when Darius pressed a finger closer to the injury. "What—*fuck*... What does that mean? For us, I mean—Jesus fuck, Darius." His leg felt like it was about to seize up in spasms, each little tic sending piercing fire through him.

"Well, if the organization meets with smugglers along this route and brings back drugs to the mainland, it means there's at least one more player involved." Darius slid his hand along the side of Gray's thigh to…maybe deliver more pain? Holy shit, the alcohol sounded good right now. "This is where Ryan's expertise comes in handy. He was always more for diplomacy and finesse than I was."

"Was he some kind of peacemaker in the Marines?" Gray gritted his teeth and released a labored breath.

Darius chuckled. "No, he was a sniper."

"I don't think diplomacy means what you think it means."

"You'd be surprised." Darius's mouth twisted up. "What I dealt with… Protection is messy and creates headlines. He was invisible. A target stops being interesting when you can't figure out who eliminated it. Great for diplomacy." He paused. "He's thinking about your future, Gray. We have a chance to secure all your futures if we shift the blame onto someone else."

"What fucking blame?" Gray panted, incredulous. "Last time I checked, we were the victims here."

"The people who did this to you won't see it that way, and I don't think you want to spend the rest of your life worrying they might come back for you."

Gray swallowed at that, and he was granted a break. Darius backed away to dig through the box of supplies.

"You can protect yourself from a slight risk," Darius said. "If they have reason to believe we're behind these killings, however, you can bank on them seeking revenge. And sooner or later, law enforcement will pull back their token protection."

"Have I mentioned your bedside manner sucks?"

"Possibly, and it's your shitty luck I'm no doctor." Darius

hummed, pulling out gauze and whatnot. "Look, knucklehead, we gotta do cleanup anyway. We've lost the war on drugs and human trafficking, but there are still battles to be won. So if we can make it look like this whole thing is a drug deal gone wrong, you will get away scot-free, and the organization behind this will have a new enemy to focus on."

Even in the haze of mind-numbing hurt, Gray saw where Darius was coming from. And Ryan. They had seen more than Gray could ever imagine, and he wasn't going to pretend to know better. The two brothers probably had reasons for not trusting the police to solve this.

"How do we do that?" Gray tried to take a calming breath.

"Willow found two locations, one less likely for smaller boats to pick up slave owners. Ryan's already reset the course."

Gray knew the last part, that Ryan had changed the boat's direction or whatever. It was on autopilot and moving pretty slowly.

"In short, we remove any evidence that we did this," Darius explained. "We set up the smugglers. We...we bury Valerie somewhere."

"What?"

As Darius applied some cream onto a sterile pad, he slid Gray a quick, amused look. "You shot her over a dozen times, knucklehead. That's not a quick bullet to the back of someone's head. That's a crime of passion."

Gray sort of lost the plot. To add more confusion, Darius was dressing his wound, though he hadn't removed the bullet, and it was getting to be too much. Gray broke out in a cold sweat from the pain.

Maybe Darius noticed, because he left the details out of things from then on. "You don't have to worry, Gray. Ry and I will get you and the boys somewhere safe, and then we'll take care of things."

There wasn't a chance in hell Gray was satisfied with that response, but it would have to do for now. He white-knuckled the armrests and clenched his jaw as Darius wrapped gauze around his thigh.

"The bullet," Gray bit out.

"It'll have to wait," Darius replied. "If your femoral artery was hit, the bullet's probably the only thing stopping you from bleeding out. I won't risk that—and you don't want me to play surgeon out here."

Okay, good talk. "I think I'll take that alcohol now," Gray whimpered.

The sun was setting as a group of islands came into view. Gray had found a secluded spot at the bow of the yacht, the area shielded by the elevated sundeck behind him. He'd showered, had every cut and scrape cleaned or dressed, and he'd been given clothes.

He'd put on a new pair of sweats, but the T-shirt had felt too foreign. He hadn't even tried it on.

With his knees tucked under his chin and his arms wrapped around his legs, he took deep breaths and let the shivers run whenever a gust of wind blew through his damp hair. A part of him felt the sliver of freedom—that this was what freedom was. But the bigger part still couldn't go there.

Some of the guys, mostly from the staff, were rejoicing and itching to reach out to their families. Ryan and Darius had been forced to cut off all communications with the mainland so they didn't risk anything; they couldn't know for certain who was listening. Not that this had tampered with the cautious excitement on board. Those guys had jumped into the pool instead and started rambling about home.

Home.

Another thing that felt foreign to Gray. And what was the point of thinking about going home when the danger wasn't over? Someway, somehow, they were going to make it look like conflict had arisen between drug smugglers and an organization that dealt in human trafficking. They were going to hide a mountain of evidence, all while making sure the schedule was followed...? Which they'd already fucked up. They'd been off course for quite some time, and now they were blowing off the pickup spot in order to make it in time to the other location.

Gray groaned internally and slipped his fingers into his hair, tugging at the ends and willing the thoughts to slow down. Or maybe willing himself to get smarter. He hadn't been the useful fighter he'd wanted to be. He felt fucking stupid. Weak, a mess, unable to help.

A few guys were preparing dinner. Wafts of spices and something grilled reached Gray when the crosswind was strong enough, and he couldn't understand how there was any laughter. He'd even heard Cole's chuckles a couple times. Or, perhaps a better question was, why wasn't Gray with them? They'd all been given the same information by now. The others weren't oblivious to the new plan and, yet, they were now hosting a fucking barbecue and laughing.

Not all of them. Some. Charlie, Owen, and Oscar had set up temporary camp at the bridge in the pilothouse with Ryan. A couple others had withdrawn to their own spots of seclusion. Not surprisingly, outdoors. It seemed no one wanted to be on the lower decks.

"We're free, motherfuckers!" someone hollered. Not for the first time.

Gray tried to grasp the feeling. *We're free. Technically, we're free. It's over*...except it wasn't.

He growled in frustration and fisted his hair harder. Stupid fucking brain.

There was no closure. No specific point where they went from dead men walking to free. No sense of victory. Linus and Milo had died for nothing, Jackie was gone, the staff guys had taken hits too, and they'd all be fucked in the head for life.

"There you are."

Gray tensed up for a second, until his mind recognized Darius's presence. He sat down next to Gray and had a glass of OJ and a plate of food with him.

"You gotta eat, knucklehead."

Gray unfolded his legs slowly and accepted the plate. The fresh bread, salad, and chicken looked good, but he had no appetite. Despite the echoing void in his stomach.

Darius dug out a pill bottle from the pocket of—shit, he was wearing jeans. That was new. Well-worn, faded blue jeans. "Your antibiotics. You can take two."

Gray took them on autopilot, suddenly focused on more shit he hadn't noticed. Darius had been injured too. There was a bandage around his non-tatted shoulder that stood out against his sun-kissed skin.

"You got hurt?" he mumbled.

Darius peered down at his shoulder, then gave a half-dismissive shake of his head. "Flesh wound. A bullet grazed me. Nothing to write home about."

Guilt hit Gray hard, and his stomach churned. "I didn't see it. I'm sorry."

Darius sighed and draped his good arm around Gray. "While you recover from this, you have to lower your expectations and allow yourself to focus on you. Otherwise, you'll go under. For chrissakes, you haven't even begun to process all this."

Recover from this... That was what Gray chose to go with. "I thought you said there's no going back to normal."

"Mm. Define normal."

Gray rolled his eyes.

"I'm serious," Darius chuckled. "No, you won't go back to who you were, Gray. But that doesn't mean you can't work through this. You'll just be different. You'll see things differently." He cleared his throat and squinted at the islands ahead of them. "You'll carry more."

Gray stared at the islands too. They looked like paradise and were just close enough to make out sandy white beaches, the edge of a small jungle, and some cliffs. The closer they got, the brighter blue the water became. Around the islands, it appeared perfectly turquoise.

"I don't feel free," he admitted softly.

Darius drew him nearer and pressed a kiss to Gray's temple. It was a weirdly affectionate gesture, but normal rules didn't apply to them. Did they? No… They'd fucked. They'd kissed. They'd shared a bed. It'd been a game and a desperate need for comfort.

Hoping Darius felt something similar, Gray released a nervous breath and set down his plate. Then he eased away from the arm around him, only to hesitantly slip his hand into Darius's instead. And the relief hit him like a wrecking ball when Darius gave his hand a squeeze and linked their fingers together. Nope, definitely no regular rules of social conduct here.

The next best thing had been when they'd had sex. It hadn't been a matter of freedom or captivity. It'd just been Darius and him. Somewhere else.

"Hey, come here." Darius scooted back a bit to be able to lean against the wall. "I have to get back to the bridge soon. We're waiting for an update from Willow, but I think we both need this first."

Need what? Confused, Gray followed with every intention of sitting next to Darius. But Darius had other plans. He adjusted their positions so Gray was between Darius's legs.

"Do you have a fever?" Gray blurted out. Because it was one thing to hold hands for a minute. A whole other to...all but cuddle.

Scratch that, it literally became cuddling the second Darius chuckled and drew Gray flush with his body. Bizarre how easy it was to ignore physical hurt when emotional warmth dripped into him like molten syrup.

"I promise you you're free, knucklehead."

Something cracked inside Gray, and he swallowed hard. He also relaxed. He sank into Darius's embrace and let out a shuddering breath. He couldn't believe it fully, that he was free, but he could put his trust in this man.

"I owe you everything." Gray's voice came out thick.

Darius exhaled a laugh and pressed his lips to the top of Gray's head. "One day, I'll tell you why I get into these situations. Then you'll know I'm the one who owes you."

Yeah, that made no fucking sense whatsoever.

Gray didn't push for an answer now, though. He dug up an ounce of humor instead. "I thought it was 'cause my stepdad pays well."

Darius's shoulders shook with silent amusement. "You didn't buy that, huh?"

A small smile played on Gray's lips as he turned carefully and rested his cheek on Darius's chest. "No, not really."

It wasn't sex or freedom or blinding desire, but it was comfort. Gray got what he craved for a moment. He was able to close his eyes and take a deep breath without fearing for his life, and he could allow himself that sliver of hope again.

Right then and there, they were somewhere else.

Just you and me.

GRAY AND DARIUS ARE BACK IN STRANDED

"If there's one thing I've learned these past few weeks, it's that I don't have to be stuck on an island to be stranded. The world has become a strange place, and I don't feel like I belong anywhere."

MORE FROM *Cara Dee*

In Camassia Cove, everyone has a story to share

Abel & Madigan
Chloe & Aiden
Willow
...along with a crossover from the Touch Series, Ryan & Angel & Greg

Cara freely admits she's addicted to revisiting the men and women who yammer in her head, and several of her characters cross over in other titles. If you enjoyed this book, you might like the following.

Power Play (M/M) Abel & Madigan. A sweet, angsty Daddy kink novel that deals with mental health disorders and the love between a hotheaded hockey player who struggles with his bipolar disorder, and an older, dominant tattoo artist. Gray is a secondary character in this book, and it takes place right before Auctioned. We also meet Darius briefly in Power Play.

Inappropriately Yours (M/F) Isla & Jack, Aiden & Chloe. Two romances in one book. Isla Roe publishes her first novel under the name her father has made famous for his own novels, but it doesn't work out as well for her. More like, it crashes and burns. Her father sends her to Washington and his college friend to get help with her writing. In the end, she finds a lot more than advice, and Aiden Roe, Isla's dad, makes a trip up to Camassia to see what's going on. That's where he runs in to his childhood crush, innkeeper and single mother of four rambunctious boys, Chloe Nolan. This is the first glimpse we get of Gray, Chloe's son.

Touch: The Complete Series (M/F, M/M/F) Everyone's getting their kink on in San Francisco. This is the complete series, consisting of seven novellas and novels, several outtakes and future takes, about men and women finding their way in BDSM. Heavy on Daddykink and other fetishes. In one of the novellas, we meet Greg Cooper, a jaded masochist who falls for the sadistic Dom Ryan Quinn and his much younger, equally sadistic wife, the switch, the baby girl, Angel Quinn. Ryan and Angel may strike hard, but their hearts are warm and open, a combination Greg finds impossible to resist.

Check out Cara's entire collection at www.caradeewrites.com, and don't forget to sign up for her newsletter so you don't miss any new releases, updates on book signings, free outtakes, giveaways, and much more.

About Cara

I'm often awkwardly silent or, if the topic interests me, a chronic rambler. In other words, I can discuss writing forever and ever. Fiction, in particular. The love story—while a huge draw and constantly present—is secondary for me, because there's so much more to writing romance fiction than just making two (or more) people fall in love and have hot sex. There's a world to build, characters to develop, interests to create, and a topic or two to research thoroughly. Every book is a challenge for me, an opportunity to learn something new, and a puzzle to piece together. I want my characters to come to life, and the only way I know to do that is to give them substance—passions, history, goals, quirks, and strong opinions—and to let them evolve. Additionally, I want my men and women to be relatable. That means allowing room for everyday problems and, for lack of a better word, flaws. My characters will never be perfect.

Wait...this was supposed to be about me, not my writing.

I'm a writey person who loves to write. Always wanderlusting, twitterpating, kinking, and geeking. There's time for hockey and cupcakes, too. But mostly, I just love to write.

Printed in Great Britain
by Amazon